CHRISTMAS WHERE SHE BELONGS

BY
MEREDITH WEBBER

MILLS
BOON

First published in Great Britain 2012
by Mills & Boon, an imprint of Harlequin (UK) Limited.
Large Print edition 2013
Harlequin (UK) Limited, Eton House,
18-24 Paradise Road, Richmond, Surrey TW9 1SR

© Meredith Webber 2012

ISBN: 978 0 263 23113 7

Harlequin (UK) policy is to use papers that are natural, renewable and recyclable products and made from wood grown in sustainable forests. The logging and manufacturing process conform to the legal environmental regulations of the country of origin.

Printed and bound in Great Britain
by CPI Antony Rowe, Chippenham, Wiltshire

Somehow Clancy was in his arms, dirt and all, and as he held her body close to his the tension drained out of him, to be replaced by a gladness he had no idea how to explain.

So he kissed her instead of trying for words—kissed her lips, her chin, her eyelids, showering kisses on her face, not daring to move lower because there was more heat in him than in the overly hot attic.

And Clancy was kissing him back, her lips finding bits of his skin, pressing against it, murmuring all the time—wordless sounds that were music to his ears.

His hands roamed across her back, feeling the flat planes of her shoulderblades, the fine, sharp bones of her spine, the padding on her backside that had teased him as he'd climbed the stairs.

'We promised Helen,' she finally reminded him, 'and anyway, this is daft. We barely know each other.'

He eased back so he could look into her face.

'I know you, Willow Clancy. You're as soft and sheltering as the tree whose name you bear, yet tenacious too, your roots deep in the earth, so you stay upright while floods rage around you. It isn't time we need in order to know about each other—you know that as well as I do, because we knew each other when we met. As if fate had worked it out. Whether that's a good thing is another matter altogether.'

Dear Reader

Christmas 2010 to January 2011 was a really tough time for many thousands of people in my home state of Queensland, Australia, as floods and a vicious cyclone devastated eighty percent of the state. Rebuilding property has taken a very long time, and rebuilding the people—especially families who lost loved ones—will take a lot longer.

Having spent a lot of time in the areas devastated by these events, I wanted this book to be a tribute to the way people who have suffered such adversity and loss heave themselves up off the ground—or out of the mud, in this case—and get on with life. Christmas must have been especially hard for many of those people, but the human spirit prevails and celebrations continue.

Mac and Clancy's story is typical of how the spirit of Christmas can help with healing, and bring joy to people who are or have been suffering. I hope you enjoy it as much as I enjoyed writing it.

Best wishes

Meredith

Meredith Webber says of herself, 'Once I read an article which suggested that Mills and Boon were looking for new Medical Romance™ authors. I had one of those "I can do that" moments, and gave it a try. What began as a challenge has become an obsession—though I do temper the "butt on seat" career of writing with dirty but healthy outdoor pursuits, fossicking through the Australian Outback in search of gold or opals. Having had some success in all of these endeavours, I now consider I've found the perfect lifestyle.'

Recent titles by Meredith Webber:

THE SHEIKH AND THE SURROGATE MUM
NEW DOC IN TOWN
ORPHAN UNDER THE CHRISTMAS TREE
MELTING THE ARGENTINE
    DOCTOR'S HEART
TAMING DR TEMPEST

**These books are also available in eBook format
from www.millsandboon.co.uk**

CHAPTER ONE

HE SHOULDN'T have brought the dog. This had occurred to him even before he'd approached the front entrance to the ultra-modern block of apartments on Brisbane's South Bank complex. But young Gracie had needed to get to hospital, and the boy up the road who usually fed the dog when he, Mac, went away, was off on holidays with his family.

In fact, just about the whole town was on holiday—down at the coast, splashing in the sea, trying to put the trauma of last year's floods behind them as they celebrated the Christmas break with family and friends.

So, he'd had to bring the dog, and it wasn't actually deliberate that he was encouraging Mike to investigate an interesting new city smell just a couple of yards from the classy-looking entrance to the apartment block.

A couple of yards from the camera he could see winking above the numbers and name plates on a panel beside the door!

Deep breath, press the buzzer, you're doing this for Hester. You loved Hester and deep down you love Mike, for all his lack of ability to learn even the most basic of dog commands.

'Heel!' he said hopefully to Mike, who'd wandered as far as his lead—well, bit of rope, really—would allow.

Mike turned around and smiled goofily at him—smiling was the one thing the dog was good at and anyone who'd seen him smile had to admit it *was* a smile.

Mac smiled back.

Clancy jumped as the sound of the front-door buzzer blasted through the small apartment.

Well, maybe not blasted, but she'd been sitting on a beanbag—*in* the beanbag—and gazing blankly at the ceiling, trying to decide if she was bored enough with the long summer break to go down and visit her mother.

'Come for Christmas,' her mother kept urging, but, much as Clancy loved her beautiful, warm, zany mother, and was fond of the group of friends who shared her mother's life in the commune, memories of the nut loaf in the shape of a turkey that had been the centrepiece of last year's Christmas dinner were still vivid in Clancy's mind.

That and the lantana flower wine.

So she'd reached the 'probably not' stage, and was just considering starting on the 'to do' list she'd written at the beginning of the holidays when the noise of the buzzer startled her. It was enough of a shock that getting out of the beanbag became more of a battle than usual—it clutched at her so that tipping it to one side and crawling out became the only option.

The buzzer sounded angry the second time, so she grabbed at the handset, dropped it, picked it up and finally peered at the picture on the small screen.

There was a pirate on her doorstep.

Or maybe he was a buccaneer—she had no idea what constituted the difference between the two. Tousled, over-long dark hair, a couple of days' beard and dark, deep-set eyes glared into the camera. His lips were moving and she could read the impatient words. 'Come on, answer the door.'

She responded to the unheard request.

'Yes?'

Hardly a welcoming 'yes', in fact a very cold, detached response, but now she was over the initial shock of having a pirate on the doorstep, her rational brain had put together the tousled hair and beard and told her it was some emissary from her mother—a fellow hippie from over the border, probably carrying a woven reed basket full of inedible cheese, green gooseberries and very hard bread.

'Miss Clancy? I'm a lawyer and I need to talk to you about an inheritance—'

He didn't look like any lawyer she'd ever seen. And unless her father had remembered he had a daughter and then died, she couldn't imagine she'd be getting an inheritance.

Actually, from the little she'd heard of her father, an inheritance was *highly* unlikely.

Piratical conman?

But why choose her?

Had he buzzed at all the doors and she was the only one who'd answered?

And wouldn't a conman look presentable, or at the very least clean shaven?

'Here, I'm holding up my ID from the hospital—I'm a doctor as well as a lawyer and I flew a patient down from Carnock early this morning so needed my ID.'

Clancy barely glanced at the name, seeing first the words 'Angel Flight' with the halo over the top of the word 'Angel'. She'd supported this charity since treating a child from the country, flown down by a volunteer pilot for a follow-up appointment after an operation. The men and women involved in the charity were doing really useful work.

Was it because of the halo that she pressed the

button to open the front door—something she never did to strangers without a far more lengthy interrogation?

Or had a certain authority in his voice overcome her usual caution?

It certainly couldn't have been the voice, for all it had made her think of rich, dark, slowly melting chocolate.

She was still pondering these alternatives—adamantly denying the last—when the front-door buzzer sounded. The man who looked like a pirate had obviously arrived.

Security conscious as she was, Clancy had the door chain in place. She opened the door the mere four inches its reach would allow, and peered through the gap at the man—more piratical than ever close up, although maybe that was the effects of the rather worn red shirt and fraying, cut-off jeans.

'What do you want?' she asked.

At least his hands were free of woven baskets.

His answer was a grin, so slight yet so cheeky, so—endearing somehow—it took her breath away.

'I've brought you your inheritance,' he said, 'but it won't fit through that small a gap.'

He turned his head and said, 'Mike!' in a very stern voice, and to Clancy's total astonishment a huge dog bounded into view, its long, thin nose poking inquisitively through the crack in the doorway.

Dumbstruck, Clancy stared at the dog—which seemed to be smiling at her.

Then anger built, slowly at first but rising to heat her entire body.

'If this is my mother's idea of a joke then it's not funny,' she growled, trying to push the dog's nose back through the door so she could slam it in the man's face. 'I live in a one-bedroom apartment that isn't big enough to swing a cat, let alone accommodate a dog the size of a small horse. I am perfectly happy living alone, I do *not* need a dog, or a cat, or a bird, not even a goldfish. I *like* living alone, and it's about time my daffy mother recognised and accepted that fact.'

The speech was slightly spoiled by the fact that she'd continued to push at the dog's muzzle, but rather than budging he seemed to be trying to ease more of his considerable length into her apartment, happily licking her hand as he did so.

'I don't actually know your mother.'

She shot upright, staring in horror at the dog, although she now realised it was the man, not the dog, who had spoken.

'May we come in?'

Still regarding the dog with suspicion and shock, Clancy opened the door.

Once inside the apartment, both the man and the dog grew bigger, taking up most of the space in her minimal living room.

'Good thing you don't do furniture or we wouldn't have fitted,' the man said, smiling cheerfully at her.

'Who *are* you?' Clancy demanded. Nerves jangled throughout her body, no doubt because she'd been stupid enough to let this stranger into her flat.

Although the jangling didn't feel like fear…

'I'm called Mac,' the man was saying, and he was holding out his hand, very politely.

It was an automatic reaction to take a hand that was held out to you, but no sooner had skin touched skin than Clancy knew she'd made a big mistake.

And confirmed the jangling had nothing to do with fear.

'I'm Clancy,' she said, snatching her hand back lest it transmit any of the rioting going on in her body. She'd heard of instant attraction, but this was ridiculous!

Mac let his gaze roam around the tiny apartment, mainly because he didn't want to keep staring at the woman. It wasn't that she was so outstandingly beautiful, but she had eyes as green as the lucerne in his back paddock—green with a hint of blue—and skin as smooth as a new baby's, ivory pale but not white, all set off, well, framed really, by a cap of feathery dark hair.

She was small, but definitely curvy, and although dressed for a relaxing Sunday at home, there was no hint of sloppiness—in fact, she was wearing long shorts with a crease that could cut your hand and a spotless, beautifully ironed T-shirt.

Who ironed T-shirts?

'You wanted something?'

The voice was good as well, soft, slightly husky, deeper than you'd expect from a smallish woman.

'Mac?' she added, when he didn't reply—couldn't really, he was lost in surprise that this should be Hester's niece.

He pulled himself together and looked around for Mike, who, wonder of wonders, was sitting by his side, pretending to be a perfect dog.

'I…' Mac began, then realised he had no idea how to go on.

'Is there somewhere we can sit?' he asked. 'I realise you must have just moved in, and don't have furniture, but I noticed coffee shops up the road with pavement tables. We could take Mike there.'

'Mike?' the woman echoed, though she obviously caught on because she was looking at the dog.

'Hester called all her dogs by people names,

which is strange when you consider she regarded dogs as far more intelligent than people.'

The woman, Miss Clancy, frowned and shook her head, then put up one hand and ruffled her neatly cut hair.

'I'm sorry,' she said, 'I haven't a clue what you're talking about, but you're right, let's go and get a coffee.'

Mac was about to head out the door when she added, rather testily, 'And not having furniture doesn't mean I've just moved in, I just haven't found the furniture I want.'

She lifted a handbag off a hook by the door and followed him out, pulling the door shut behind her, but before they reached the elevator, an elderly man emerged from another apartment, obviously heading in the same direction, though he paused to give Mike a disapproving look.

'Dogs are not allowed in this building. You should know that, Miss Clancy.'

'He's just passing through, Mr Bennett,' Clancy responded politely, though the colour in her cheeks suggested she was embarrassed by the reprimand.

Mac waited until they were outside the complex, walking up the tree-lined street towards the closest pavement café, before bringing up the subject again.

'So, it's going to be a problem, you inheriting Mike?'

The only response was a narrow-eyed glare, but even glaring those eyes were special.

They reached the café and Clancy chose a table at the outside edge of the pavement, no doubt assuming it would keep Mike out of other patrons' way. But she didn't know Mike.

'So!' she said, sitting down with her back to the quiet road. 'Start at the beginning, who you are, why are you here, who is or was Hester and, probably most important of all, as I can't keep the dog, what are you going to do with him?'

He smiled at her.

'Very succinct summation of the main points. No wonder you've done so well as a teacher,' he said.

The smile was Clancy's undoing. It sneaked through her skin and curdled in her blood, turning it thick and sluggish, but no matter how her body was behaving, she couldn't let him get away with the jibe.

'I am a nurse educator, the senior lecturer in surgical nursing and theatre skills at the university,' she pointed out.

The man's smile widened.

'Just as I said—a really good teacher! You must be to have done so well. But tell me, having trained to nurse, what made you go into teaching? Did you not like nursing?'

He was impossible.

'I don't think that's any of your business,' she snapped. 'Anyway, we're here to talk about the dog, not me.'

'Ah, Mike!' the infuriating man drawled, while the dog sniffed the leg of a leggy blonde three tables away and was rewarded with a bit of buttered and very jammy croissant.

Should she call the dog? Clancy wondered. Would it come if she did?

'Start with who you are,' she said to the man, deciding it was easier to ignore the dog.

'My name is McAlister Warren, and—'

'McAlister Warren? That sounds more like a firm of lawyers than a name.'

Yes, that had been rude, but she was strung so tightly the words had just slipped out. Anyway, the situation was so bizarre, surely a little rudeness wouldn't count.

Not that rudeness affected the man. He could give as good as he got.

'It's the name my parents gave me,' he said smoothly, 'and coming from someone called Willow Cloud Clancy, your criticism of my name is a bit rich.'

Clancy cringed. Few people knew her real name, and those who did would never dare to use it. She'd been Clancy from her first day at school—at real school, that was…

'Everyone calls me Clancy,' she said, aware that colour had crept into her face. He was right—she should *never* have mentioned names.

'Good choice,' he said, smiling cheerfully at

her across the table and causing the little hairs on her arms to stand on end as if his words had brushed her skin. 'Now, coffee? Something to eat with it?'

Clancy had been so busy trying to work out why the man was affecting her, she hadn't noticed the waitress, one she didn't know, approach the table.

'Long, black and nothing to eat,' she managed to reply, hoping coffee—black—might get her brain working again while certain that the way she felt, she'd choke on food.

'So, you're Mac,' she prompted. 'From Carnock, was it?'

As she said the word, a memory stirred and she knew why she'd opened the door. Once, long ago, she'd searched for a town called Carnock on a map in the school library, wondering just how far away it was and whether she could walk there if she started early enough. She was a good walker, and every morning walked a long way uphill to catch the bus to school...

'You've heard of Carnock?'

Mac's question was casual enough, but Clancy could feel his attention was focussed fully on her, as if the question had some deeper meaning.

'One of the towns that had to be totally evacuated during the floods last year?' she responded, realising she hadn't connected the town to her childhood memory back then. It had to be the talk of an inheritance that had triggered the memory now.

Although, back when she *had* set out to walk there, and the search parties had returned her to the hippie commune that had been home, her mother had told her that while her father might have lived there once, it was the last place on earth he'd have gone back to—a place he'd hated.

'And that's all you know of it?' Mac persisted.

Clancy frowned at him.

'It might have been the town my father came from, but as I never really knew him, and as my mother always said he wouldn't be seen dead in the place ever again, I doubt you've come to tell me he *is* dead. Although...' she looked across to where Mike was now being offered bacon and egg at a far table '…leaving me a dog would be consistent with his complete lack of presence in my life.'

'You know nothing of him?' Mac asked.

'He went away—that's all I know. All my mother would ever say. I was two, maybe three—' She broke off suddenly, shrugged, then added, 'Actually, having escaped the commune and my mother's hippie lifestyle as soon as I possibly could, I can't find it in my heart to blame him.'

Mac turned her words over in his head, but found no bitterness in them. How sad that all she knew of her father was that he'd gone away. How hurtful it must have been for her, growing up with that knowledge.

But he was on a mission and couldn't afford to be distracted by this woman's unhappy child-hood—if it *had* been unhappy.

'The thing is, your father did come from Car-nock and, no, he didn't turn up dead there—in fact, as far as Hester was able to ascertain, he's still alive—but he is, in her opinion, a total waste

of space and you probably didn't miss much not
having him around.'

Clancy didn't look convinced, but at least she
was intrigued enough to ask, 'And exactly who
was Hester?'

'Hester Clancy was your great-aunt, and an ut-
terly wonderful woman. Every small town has
someone like Hester, but Carnock was blessed
with the best. Hester was the person young girls
went to when they discovered they were pregnant, she was the person battered women eventually talked to, she'd find the money to send the
clever kids in town to university when their parents couldn't afford it, and after the floods she
had three families living in her house for nearly
a year while their homes were rebuilt.

'She fought insurance companies and the flood-
fund people to get the best deal for all of them,
and practically forced tradesmen to work in Carnock when they could all be getting better money
in the nearby mines.'

'Wonder Woman, in fact,' Clancy muttered,

and although there was no meanness in the re-mark, Mac couldn't let it slide.

'Not really. Just caring, and giving, and very, very sensible.' He paused, then had to add, 'I imagine you've got the same sensible gene. Small apartment close to where you work, waiting until you can afford to buy good furniture rather than spending foolishly on rubbish—'

'I can buy furniture whenever I like,' Clancy retorted, the flash of fire in the green eyes sug-gesting she'd been called sensible before and hated it.

'I'm sure you can,' he soothed, but he couldn't resist smiling, and slowly, reluctantly, she smiled back, her whole face lighting up, the radiance doing something to his lungs so his breath lodged in a lump in his trachea.

'So, Hester the wonder woman left me a dog?'

Had she, too, felt whatever it was that had zapped between them? After a silence that seemed to stretch for ever, she'd thrown him a question to get the conversation back on track.

'And the house the dog lives in,' he told her, glad to be back on track himself.

No smile now, just total bewilderment, although she did recover enough to ask, 'The house with the three flood families living in it?'

'No, no, they've all moved out,' he assured her. 'At the moment I'm your only tenant, although I must admit I don't pay much rent—none, in fact. Hester took me in after the flood as well, but I've stayed on. She wasn't well, you see, and the house is old and needed a lot of maintenance—'

'Stop right there!'

Clancy actually held up her hand to halt his explanation, and the waitress bringing the coffee stopped obligingly. By the time they'd sorted that out, and had coffee on the table, Mac had forgotten what he'd been saying, mainly because Clancy had smiled again and although it had been at the waitress, not at him, the smile had still caused problems in his chest.

Now Clancy lifted her coffee cup, pursing her lips to sip from it, and Mac felt a judder in his heart. No way. This wasn't happening. He didn't

do instant attraction. Both his long-term partner-
ships had been gradual, cautious involvements—
and as both of them had failed, how much more
disastrous would a relationship based on nothing
more than physical attraction be?

Relationship?

Where *was* his head?

'Start again with you, McAlister,' Clancy was
saying. 'At the door you said you were a lawyer,
then you show a hospital ID with "Angel Flight"
on it, which I know doesn't make you a doctor
because you could just be a pilot with a plane,
but none of this explains why were you sponging
off this Hester until she died. Were you hoping
to get the house and dog yourself?'

'Heaven forbid!' he retorted, pleased the woman's accusation had cleared his head—if not his
chest. 'The place is falling down. I just didn't
want to leave her on her own. Also, it's a good
house, and has historical value, and it deserves
to live. But so much needs doing to it. I could
only keep things going, getting a tradesperson
in when necessary, although I've become a dab

hand at changing tap washers and cleaning blocked drains.'

'That's not making anything clearer,' Clancy told him as she battled to make sense of the situation. She didn't know if it was what he was saying or because of her reaction to him as a man, but for whatever reason every time the man spoke she grew more confused. 'What are you really? A doctor, a lawyer, a carpenter, odd-job man…?'

The man had the hide to laugh and Mike, apparently hearing the sound, came trotting across, grinning his stupid grin, a little bit of bacon dangling from the beard beneath his chin.

The dog nuzzled his head beneath Mac's hand and as Mac's long fingers rubbed the dog's head Clancy had the weirdest sensation that the fingers were touching her—rubbing *her* head, and ruffling *her* hair.

'A doctor first. The lawyer and odd-job man are part-time jobs, like the farming. It probably won't surprise you to know that although doctors are desperately needed in country areas across Queensland, the only lawyering the locals need is the odd will or a bit of conveyancing when they buy or sell something.'

'Farming? Did you sneak farming in there as well?' Clancy asked. 'Law and medicine are both long degrees, and then there's articles for a lawyer and internship for a doctor. So that makes you, what—a hundred and ten years old?'

'I am thirty-six,' Mac replied, somewhat stiffly, Clancy felt. 'And for your information I started studying law, then switched to medicine after four years. After I moved to Carnock I finished my law degree as an external student and did the practical legal training course to get my practicing certificate.'

'Okay, so you're the town doctor *and* the town lawyer and you live in my house, which is falling down. Is that it?'

'More or less.' The reply this time was grumpy, to say the least. 'Although it isn't your house, it's Mike's.'

'Mike's?'

The word came out as a yelp, which won an answering yelp from the dog himself, who shifted his allegiance from Mac to her.

Clancy stared at the man who had, in less than an hour, turned her neatly ordered life completely upside down.

'Can a dog inherit a house? Own a house? Are you sure that's legal?'

She patted Mike's head to show she had nothing against him personally, and, apparently liking that, he rested his chin on her leg, liberally smearing her clean white cargo shorts with dog slobber.

'Life tenancy,' Mac responded, 'after which it reverts to you, but—'

Up to this point, the man had been looking at her as he explained things—in fact, he'd been looking at her so intently she'd felt uncomfortable, although that could have been the attraction thing. Now, not only had he left an ominous-sounding 'but' dangling at the end of his sentence, but McAlister Whoever was gazing over her left shoulder—towards the road behind them, not looking at her at all…

'But?'

'Well…'

The man was hedging.

'Actually,' he began again, 'to get the house, you have to take the dog.'

'Actually,' Clancy mimicked, 'having heard about the house, I doubt very much I'd want it, while as for the dog—'

Unfortunately, perhaps understanding he was the dog in question, Mike looked up at her at that moment…and smiled.

No! No way! You do *not* disrupt your carefully planned life because a dog smiled at you!

'Couldn't the dog be mine in name but continue to live in the house with you?'

The man *did* look at her now, studying her for what seemed an inordinate length of time before answering—only what he said wasn't an answer at all.

'I can understand you haven't much time for your father, but have you no curiosity at all about him, about his family, your forebears? Wouldn't you at least like to see the town, look at the house?'

The nut roast had looked more like a dinosaur than a turkey, Clancy remembered, an image of the monstrosity flashing through her brain. While as for the wine…

Now here was the perfect excuse *not* to go to Nimbin for Christmas. The summer break was three months long—she could visit Carnock for a couple of weeks and still have plenty of time to complete her 'to do' list.

And though she was reluctant to admit it, the man was right, she *did* have a good deal of curiosity about her father. She'd just left it packed away in the cellar of her mind since her abortive attempt to find him back when she'd been a child.

'I don't have a car. Is there a bus, or a train?' she asked, and Mac frowned at her.

'You don't have a car?'

She frowned right back at him.

'You make it sound as if it's a sin against humanity—have you not heard of minimising your personal carbon footprint? And why would I need a car? A pleasant stroll across the pedestrian bridge over the river takes me to work and the city, I have parklands all around me, I have a bicycle if I want to go further afield. So, no, I don't have a car.'

'Well, you could fly back out there with me. I'm going this afternoon and I'm almost sure to be coming back down before too long. Otherwise someone in town could give you a lift.'

He paused, again studying her a little too intently.

'You'll come?' he added.

She thought of her eight-year-old self setting out to walk to the place called Carnock, the page she'd torn from the atlas in the school library folded in her pocket, and suddenly the idea of seeing the town she'd been headed for all those years ago filled her with an excitement she hadn't felt for a long, long time.

'I'll come!' she said, and she scratched Mike's head, ruffling the rough hair on it.

CHAPTER TWO

ASKING for trouble, that's what it was, encouraging her to visit Carnock. But who'd have expected Hester's great-niece to look the way she did? Obviously as sensible and capable as Hester had been, yet somehow vulnerable at the same time.

On the other hand, it was only fair she see the house before she made any decision, Mac reminded himself.

Her attention was focussed on Mike at the moment, so he could study her without making it too obvious. Not that he hadn't been studying her ever since they'd met, trying to analyse the unexpected physical bond he'd felt from the moment he'd laid eyes on her.

Maybe there was a look of Hester about her, but if there was he couldn't see it. And as far as women were concerned, his preference was for blondes, and long-haired blondes at that. This woman with her gamine looks and hair like a pixie's cap—she just wasn't his type.

'You said "fly back" with you. You have a plane?'

She'd looked up and caught him staring at her, embarrassing him enough to launch him into speech.

'Cessna 172, handy little plane, four seater, has a range of about a thousand k...' He stopped and smiled at her. 'You don't really want to know all that, do you? But, yes, I have a plane.'

'I've never flown,' she said, the vulnerable part of her looks coming to the fore.

'Never flown in a small plane?'

Well, a lot of people hadn't!

'Not flown at all,' she said. 'Early on I didn't have the money for expensive holidays and now—I don't know, I guess I just haven't got around to planning one.'

Instinct told him there was more to *that* story but he wouldn't pursue it now.

'You'll enjoy it. It's only a couple of hours'

flight, three at the most. The weather's great, and we go over pretty country—the Great Dividing Range and the Downs. It will be all green and gold at the moment with either new crops planted or the last of the sunflowers. Now to plans. I want to call in and say hello to my parents while I'm in town. How long will you take to pack? How about I collect you at one?'

She was shaking her head, a stunned look on her face, then her lips tightened and she gave a final head shake.

'It's not that I don't trust you, but how do I even know you're who you say you are? I mean, I know it's highly unlikely someone would choose me to abduct because I'm worth nothing as a hostage. But I've known you, what, a couple of hours at most? And now you expect me to hop in a small plane with you and fly off to a place I've barely heard of.'

'Ah, but you *had* heard of it, that's the point. I suspect that's why you let me in, when every-thing about you tells me you're a very cautious person. I don't blame you for feeling apprehensive. Look…' He fished in his pocket for his wallet and, pulling it out, produced a rather squashed card. 'The hospital number is there—phone the hospital and ask any questions you need to ask. Being Sunday, Annabelle Crane, our—'

'Annabelle Crane—beautiful blonde with a sexy laugh and a never-ending stream of terrible jokes?' Clancy spoke in what she hoped was a light-hearted voice, although the mention of Annabelle's name had started heart palpitations.

Bad heart palpitations!

'You know Annabelle?'

Fighting an urge to press her hand to her chest, Clancy said carefully, 'I trained with her, but I lost touch after she married. You said she's Annabelle *Crane*? She's not married now?'

Not married to James?

Forget James. The question she needed to ask herself was could she face Annabelle again as if nothing had ever happened?

The palpitations were so bad she seriously considered telling Mac to keep the inheritance and get out of her life, but the name of that town—

Carnock—kept echoing in her head, while memories of a man who'd tossed her in the air as a child…

And James falling out of love with her and into love with Annabelle hadn't *really* been Annabelle's fault, any more than James using the overseas honeymoon bookings he'd made for himself and her—the insensitivity of which had caused Clancy the most pain—could be blamed on Annabelle…

And the pirate wondered why she'd never flown anywhere.

'Definitely not married.' Mac's reply dragged her out of the past. He spoke casually, but Clancy heard a hint of something behind the words. Were he and Annabelle an item? Why did he put so much stress on the word 'definitely'?

'They must have split up,' Clancy said, telling herself it was none of her business if Annabelle and Mac *were* involved, and that the uneasiness in her stomach was nothing more than to be expected, given how her life had shifted in the last couple of hours.

'Do you want to phone her?' he said, offering his mobile. 'The hospital is on speed dial, just press two.'

Clancy studied the phone—a much better idea than studying the man. But taking it, pressing the number two, would show a level of distrust she no longer felt. Hadn't really felt at all with this man from the moment she'd seen his picture in the camera by the door.

Which was stupid.

But taking the phone, pressing two, would put her onto Annabelle...

You're over it! You moved on years ago!

She took the phone and pressed the number two, wondering at the same time who would answer if she pressed one instead.

Annabelle?

'Carnock Hospital, Annabelle speaking. That you, Mac?'

Clancy pressed the button that cut off the call and handed the phone back to Mac, whose hand closed over it just as it began to ring. He glanced at the number displayed and somehow stopped the noise without answering, instead slipping the phone back into his shirt pocket.

'You didn't want to chat with Annabelle? Catch up on what's happening? Share a few student reminiscences?' he asked, though it was apparent he hadn't wanted to speak to Annabelle either, for who else would have been phoning right then?

Now she studied the man, a move aimed at distracting her mind from the reminiscences that lay between her and Annabelle!

Scruffy, that's what he was, yet it was a very appealing scruffiness, maybe because of the twinkle that was almost always evident in his dark brown eyes.

It was dangerous, that twinkle, something to beware of, so she ignored it, *and* the teasing note in his voice, and answered as coolly as her overheated and still-jolted body would allow.

'I imagine we can catch up in Carnock,' she said, although catching up with Annabelle had never been high on her wish list for the future.

'You will, at that,' Mac assured her.

Some assurance!

'So, one o'clock!' Clancy said, knowing she had to get away right now, before the clashing chaos of attraction and memories had her disintegrating into a twisted mass of nerves on the footpath. 'I need to pack,' she added as she stood up, knocking over her chair in her haste. 'It'll be hot, I imagine.'

She bent to pick up the chair but Mac was before her, his hand brushing hers as she grabbed at it, his quiet 'Let me' suggesting he'd somehow read the turmoil inside her.

And now they were both bent, heads close together, gazes locked, something shimmering in the air between them, something that definitely wasn't distrust...

Mike saved the day, leaping over the fallen chair and knocking over the table.

Clancy had to laugh. The dog was sitting in the middle of the shambles, grinning his idiotic grin.

'Well, I'm glad someone's laughing,' Mac growled, as he righted the table. 'You go and pack. I'll settle up for the damage before I kill your dog.'

'You brought him here,' Clancy reminded him, and Mac sighed.

'Indeed I did,' he said, and Clancy couldn't miss the regret in his voice.

She slipped away, thinking not of Annabelle Crane and James but of whether Mac's regret was for bringing the dog to the city, or was it for getting himself involved with her?

Although they were hardly involved—he was a lawyer who had contacted the beneficiary of a will, and she was the beneficiary. It was purely a business meeting.

Maybe!

Packing took all of fifteen minutes, cleaning out the refrigerator and giving her next-door neighbour the perishables another ten, which left Clancy with two hours and twenty-two minutes to fill before one o'clock.

She considered using the time to contact her mother, a process that could take easily that long as it involved contacting a neighbour who had a phone, who then raised a flag to indicate there was a message for someone in the commune. It could be that the flag wouldn't be seen for hours. Or days.

And if days, she'd be gone before her mother phoned back, and then she'd worry when she couldn't get hold of Clancy, so all in all it was better to write.

Two hours and eighteen minutes—decisions didn't take up much time.

Well, sitting around was no good because then she'd start thinking, and if she started thinking she'd regret making the impulsive decision. She *never* made impulsive decisions, knowing they invariably led to loss of control, and being in control was the mainstay of her life.

Or had been for some time...

She found some paper and began the letter, telling her mother of the unexpected appearance of Great-Aunt Hester in the family tree, and the strange bequest.

I'm not going because I still hanker for a father, she wrote, although as she put the words on paper, she wondered if they were entirely true, *but because this woman left me her house and*

*dog in good faith, so the least I can do is have a
look at the situation, sum it up and make a decision.*

There, that sounded sensible. No need to mention Annabelle Crane being in Carnock.

Sometimes Clancy thought her mother regret-
ted the break-up with James more than she herself did. But hadn't it been the shock of James's
visit to the commune, and meeting her mother's
extraordinary friends, that had started the disin-
tegration of their relationship...?

Determined not to dwell on the past, she finished the letter and went into the alcove in her
bedroom that she thought of as her office. Once
there, she was able to lose herself in the first item
on her 'to do' list, the preparation of lectures for
the following year. She wanted to make them
more challenging, particularly for the first-year
students, so they would get a feel for the job they
were training to do.

So, of course, rather than waiting by the front
door at one o'clock, she was lost in Lecture Two
when the buzzer buzzed.

Shoving her laptop into its case, she slung it over her shoulder, grabbed the small bag with her belongings, and her handbag, and hit the button to allow Mac and Mike entrance to the lobby. 'I'll be right down,' she said into the intercom, and raced down the stairs, knowing it would be faster than taking the elevator.

Flushed from her downward dash, she arrived in the lobby to find Mike in trouble again, this time from a tenant Clancy didn't know, a woman who'd emerged from the elevator with a Siamese cat on a lead.

'He likes cats,' Mac was saying to the woman, who'd grabbed her pet from beneath Mike's smiling face and was glowering at Mac.

'Dogs are not allowed in this building,' the woman said, and she stalked out the door.

Mike let her go, discovering Clancy instead and rushing up to her to greet her with his front paws on her chest, so with the weight of her baggage she'd have gone flying if Mac hadn't slung his arm around her to steady her.

The area of skin beneath the clothes that

touched that arm prickled with awareness, then the arm dropped away, while Clancy battled an urge to run straight back up the stairs.

Control!

'Does he cause trouble wherever he goes?' she asked, determined to ignore her reactions to the man, and looking at Mike, who was now sitting in front of her doing a perfect dog act.

'Everywhere!' Mac said in a despairing voice, but Clancy heard the smile behind the words and understood that Mac loved the silly animal, just as Great-Aunt Hester must have.

Great-Aunt Hester—just thinking about the woman gave Clancy a weird sensation in her stomach.

She had family! Real family! Or at least she had done...

Of course, she'd always known her mother had family, somewhere down south, maybe in Victoria, but her mother's insistence that the fellow members of the commune were the only family she wanted or needed had meant Clancy had never known any of them. Which, by and large, had been okay.

Mac had taken her belongings and she was following him out the front door towards an ancient, battered, rusting four-wheel drive while she considered all of this. But as he stowed her bags in the back and opened the rear door for Mike, Clancy realised there was one question she hadn't asked and probably should have.

With her hand on the doorhandle, she turned to Mac.

'How did you find me?'

'I didn't,' he said, with a grin that seemed to light up whatever little corner of the world he was currently inhabiting. 'Hester found you. I have a feeling she had some kind of agent look into it.'

'An agent? You mean a private detective? She had someone following me?'

The grin turned into a laugh so the dark eyes sparkled with devilment.

'I very much doubt you were followed,' he assured her, taking her hand off the doorhandle and opening it for her. 'As far as I know, most things can be discovered just sitting in an office using a computer. All births are registered, you'd be on a voting register, there'd be school and university records, and a smart agent could probably even find out which dentist you went to.'

Clancy had ducked past him to get into the car, but turned back to face him, horrified by what he was saying yet knowing it was probably true.

'You think that's what happened?'

'Almost sure of it,' Mac said, then he touched her cheek. 'We're all in the same boat, about as anonymous as a pop star. Every time you go for a job, someone is finding out all this stuff about you.'

Clancy wanted to argue, but she knew everything he'd said was true, no matter how uncomfortable it might make her feel. So now she had to wonder just how much this 'agent' Mac spoke of *had* dug up. And was the information floating around the house where Mac now lived alone— apart from Mike?

Did it matter?

Deciding it didn't, she finally climbed into the

car. She was going out to see the house. Yes, she'd probably see Annabelle, but that was okay, they'd been quite good friends through university, and beyond all that a little flutter of excitement threading along her nerves reminded her she was finally going to see the place called Carnock, and maybe, just maybe, find out a little more about her father.

Unfortunately, as Mac got behind the wheel and the flutter along her nerves grew stronger, she had to wonder if it was the thought of seeing Carnock causing it, or this man she didn't know.

She'd had flutters aplenty with James in the beginning, although flutters seemed to die natural deaths as a relationship progressed, for which she'd been profoundly grateful. She had to hope, if Mac was causing the flutters, that they would also die away when a relationship *didn't* exist.

Mac was driving out through the inner suburbs, explaining that he flew in and out of Archerfield, where he kept this vehicle for his convenience when he was in Brisbane.

'There are any number of old cars like this

around an airfield. A lot of pilots are tinkerers, playing with their planes and doing up old cars—the two go together. It's fortunate for me as there's an old man out there who loves this vehicle, so although it looks as if it's coming apart at the seams, he keeps it in good running order for me.'

'And are you a tinkering pilot?' Clancy asked.

'Definitely not. I have no idea what goes on inside any engine, although I had to learn enough about the plane to be able to see anything that was obviously wrong with it. But we've a good mechanic in Carnock and I have it serviced down here every year. I just wanted to be able to get about, and in the bush a small plane's the answer.'

The conversation lagged, and although the silence wasn't uncomfortable, Clancy felt obliged to break it.

Or it may have been because she liked Mac's voice, the rich chocolate of it, that she asked, 'And your involvement with Angel Flight?'

'Ah,' Mac said, 'that's one great charity. Very few overheads, most of the work done by volunteers, and it's one thing that is of real benefit to country people all over Australia. You know about it?'

He turned towards her and Clancy smiled, glad she could answer honestly.

'I've supported it as a charity for years and I'm a registered "earth angel", but only as a hospital visitor. Having a full-time job and not having a car means I can't do hospital transfers, but when people have to stay down for any length of time, I'm put in touch with them.'

'So we have something in common apart from Hester,' Mac said, and when he smiled she *knew* the flutters were Mac-generated, although the name Carnock still gave her a thrill when she whispered it in her mind.

Thrills—flutters—what was happening to calm, sensible, in-control Willow Cloud Clancy? The girl who'd fled the drifting, laid-back, disorganised life of the commune to build a normal, stable life for herself—planned and controlled to the last detail...

This time she let the silence linger, her head

too busy puzzling over her reactions to Mac to be bothered with small talk.

But no amount of thinking came up with any reason why this particular man, of all the men she'd met in recent years, should affect her with flutters.

Surely it had to be more than a quick, bold grin and twinkling eyes and a piratical beard and tousled black hair…

Was she having second thoughts? Mac wondered. Would she get to Archerfield, take one look at his little plane, and grab a taxi to take her back to the security of her tiny apartment and her ordered life?

He knew enough about her childhood in the hippie commune—Hester's agent had been far more thorough than he'd let on—to guess she needed order in her life and some measure of control over it, but surely she could find order of a different kind in Carnock.

It was a thought that made him think again—did he *want* her living in Carnock?

The answer came immediately—a positive response. At least, he amended to himself, until he'd had a chance to get to know her, and maybe understand the attraction he felt towards her.

Once understood it would be easy to counter—

That thought stopped as abruptly as he stopped the car at the lights at Rocklea.

'Archerfield's just up the road,' he said, to break his train of thought more than the silence.

'I can see planes already,' his passenger said, and the soft, husky voice feathered up his spine, suggesting the attraction might grow instead of lessening...

Far better if she *didn't* stay!

Once airborne it was easier. He could pretend flying the little gem of a plane was a complex procedure. But even pretending, he couldn't miss the cries of delight from his passenger, who pointed out every dam and paddock and small hill as they flew towards the great range that ran down the east coast of Australia.

Enchantment shone in her face, and her delight was so open and enthusiastic that Mac found himself forgetting his pretence about the complexities of flying and joining in, naming the places they flew over, deviating off route to show her deep, uninhabited valleys in the ranges, and fields of sunflowers—faces up to the sun and so to them—ranging across the downs.

Turning north towards Carnock, he pointed out the small beginnings of the river that had caused much of the flooding the previous year.

'But it's barely a creek,' Clancy protested, and Mac explained how the ground had been waterlogged from previous rain, and the little stream already breaking its banks in places before the deluge that caused the flood had hit the town.

'Is there still visible damage in the town?' she asked, and he hesitated.

'If you'd known the town, then you'd see a difference. Some places that were washed away will never be rebuilt, but it's the invisible damage that I worry about.'

'The people?' she asked quietly, and he nodded.

'There's far too much of a "she'll be right, mate" attitude in the country,' he said. 'People—

men *and* women but particularly the men—hide their emotions in case it's seen as a weakness.'

'At least that's never a problem where I come from,' she responded. 'The nights I've fallen asleep listening to a litany of someone's revelations of their deep inner angst. But I can understand people would be scarred by the experience of the floods. Even seeing the news coverage had me in tears.'

'Carnock was lucky in that there was no loss of life, although we all thought Mike was gone. He leapt into the water when a big ball floated past—the dog's a sucker for a ball. But he arrived back home five days later. Wet and bedraggled and absolutely starving, but still as bold as ever.'

Clancy turned to pat the dog, who was lying behind the two front seats. The image of a wet, bedraggled Mike had slunk into her heart and for all she told herself she couldn't get too attached to this dog, she had a bad feeling she'd be unable to resist.

Could she get enough rent for her apartment to lease a house in the suburbs—somewhere on the train line so she wouldn't need a car? With a good yard, of course—

A jangling noise erupted through the small cabin.

'Is that your mobile?' she asked Mac, and knew the answer when she saw him fish it out of his pocket.

'Mac!' he said, while Clancy marvelled that right up here in the air the man still had mobile coverage.

Although now Mac's end of the conversation snagged her attention.

'How long ago? Is it just his ankle? Did he hit his head at all? Land on his back? Can he move his toes and fingers? Jess, Jess, stop crying. I'll be there in half an hour, maybe less. Your strip's clear? No cattle in that paddock? Okay, just make him comfortable and come down to the strip to meet me. Yes, I can take you into town. Now stop crying, take deep breaths, think of the baby, make yourself a cup of tea, then drive down to meet us.'

'Problem?' Clancy asked.

'Fellow on a property some distance from town. He's come off his motorbike, but apparently only injured his ankle. They ride around on those darned things with sandals on, would you believe, and never wear helmets. It's a wonder more farmers aren't injured.'

Was that all he was going to tell her?

Not that she needed to know more, but she'd sensed Mac had more to say.

A long sigh confirmed her guess.

'Rod's wife, Jess, is eight months pregnant. She's a city girl and although she's adapted well to country life, something like this will have thrown her.'

Not knowing what to say, Clancy waited.

'They live an hour's drive from town.'

The information was coming in dribs and drabs and although she now *knew* it was leading somewhere, she had no idea where.

'I don't want her driving into town in her condition. She's upset enough as it is, so…'

Mac turned so Clancy could see his face and

read the concern in his eyes, plus what looked like a little uncertainty lurking around his lips.

'Rod's a big man and Jess is huge at the moment so I can't fit you all in the plane. Would you be okay with me dropping you and Mike at the farm? That way you can drive into town, and Jess will have a car available to drive back home—drive Rod back home as well if it's a simple break and I can set it. Best of all, I can have Jess stay in the hospital with Rod overnight and keep an eye on her in case the stress has affected the pregnancy.'

Clancy barely heard the justifications for the scheme Mac was proposing, having stalled on the first part.

'You want me to drive these people's vehicle into town?' she demanded. 'From a place I don't know to a town I don't know?'

She didn't add 'in a car I don't know', in case that made her sound altogether too wimpish.

'Oh, that's easy,' Mac assured her. 'You go down their drive to the front gate and turn left. There's only one road and it leads to Carnock.'

There was a pause, as if something had just occurred to him, and after what seemed like too long a silence he added, 'You *can* drive?'

'Of course I can,' Clancy replied, not adding that although she had a licence she'd never made much use of it, never having owned a car, not even an old bomb, while she'd been a student. *Some* of the ethos of her childhood had stuck.

'That's good. Now, look out the window and see if you can see a house. There should be a name—Thornside—painted on the roof.'

Clancy spotted it ten minutes later, pointing it out to Mac, who circled it, gradually bringing the plane lower and lower until Clancy could see the cleared strip of a runway ahead of them, then— bump!—they were down. Mac taxied the little plane towards a huge four-wheel-drive vehicle parked beside a small shed.

'Let it be an automatic,' she prayed beneath her breath while Mac stopped the engine and yelled at Mike to sit.

Mike was already over on Clancy's knee, obviously determined to be the first out, but he did sit, all ten stone of him by the feel of things.

'Can I open the door?' Clancy asked, and Mac assured her she could. She unlatched it and pushed it open so Mike could leap out, heading straight for the pregnant woman.

Fearing he might jump up on her and knock her over, Clancy yelled his name, and to her surprise he turned around and gave his goofy smile then proceeded to ignore the woman, turning his attention instead to three farm dogs who'd also come to greet the new arrivals.

Mac introduced Clancy to Jess, who repeated the name with surprise.

'Clancy? It's your first name, or your surname? Are you related to Hester?'

'Small town,' Mac said drily, and Clancy knew exactly what he meant. Everyone would know everyone else's business.

'It's my surname but I've been called Clancy for ever. Apparently I'm Hester's great-niece, although I've only now heard of her existence.'

'Oh, you missed out on a treat! Not that Hester ever thought much of me. She believed country men should marry country women, not city slickers like me—although once she knew I was pregnant she warmed up a bit, greeting me at the shops and always asking how I was.'

Jess patted her bump, then allowed Mac to help her back into the high-set vehicle. He'd opened the back door and as Mike had already leapt in, Clancy followed.

Mac drove the short distance to where lights flickered through the leaves of a well-maintained garden, asking Jess about her husband's injury, reassuring the woman that all would be well.

'How about you make us a cuppa?' he said, as they walked up the steps to the wide front veranda. 'I could do with one, and I'm sure Clancy could as well.'

He dropped back to murmur to Clancy, 'Would you go with her and keep an eye on her?'

Clancy followed Jess obediently down a long hallway, hearing Mac's voice as he greeted his patient, looking around at the rooms that led off the passage, thinking how cool the big house was, although the heat of the day had lingered out at the airstrip.

'He'll be all right, I know that,' Jess said as Clancy entered the huge kitchen with a table big enough to seat a dozen people. 'It was just the shock of seeing him when he came home. He was white as a ghost and fainted dead away as he tried to get off the bike, then he wouldn't lean on me to get into the house.'

Jess was still shocked by her husband's injury, that much was obvious, yet she was efficiently making a big pot of tea, setting out mugs and even producing a large fruit cake from the pantry.

'I made the Christmas cake early and then de-cided to make a few more so we could enjoy it be-fore Christmas as well as after it,' she explained as she cut off slabs and put them onto plates.

'Good thinking,' Clancy said, deciding that Hester's judgement had been right—this city girl was settling well into the country.

Jess set everything on a tray and led the way out a side door and along a back veranda to where

Mac was bent over a tall young man, chatting easily as he bound the injured ankle.

'I'll X-ray it when we get to town,' Mac explained to Jess, 'but I think it might be bad enough to send him somewhere to have it pinned or it could cause problems later. Your family's in Brisbane? Would you prefer going there or would Toowoomba do?'

Jess turned to Rod.

'What do you want?' she said, and when his only reply was a broad smile, she answered Mac.

'Toowoomba's closer, he'll probably see a specialist there more quickly, and we'll be back home sooner,' she said, and Rod reached out and took her hand, the connection between the couple so obvious Clancy felt the warm glow of reflected love, and maybe just a twinge of envy.

'That's settled, then,' Mac declared. 'I'll take you back to town, X-ray it and start making arrangements. Jess, is there a neighbour you can phone to feed the dogs while you're away?'

'I'll put them on their chains now, and phone from Carnock when we know for certain we have to go to Toowoomba,' Jess replied, then she smiled at Mac. 'It's not that I'm doubting your diagnostic skills, but it just *might* be a simple break!'

'Fair enough,' Mac said, gulping down his tea and picking up the plate that held his cake. 'Can you pop this into a paper bag so I can take it with me? I seem to remember your fruit cake won first prize in last year's show, putting several older local noses out of joint.'

Jess went off happily and Mac turned to Clancy.

'Do you think you could help me get Rod out to the car? You stand on his left side and I'll take the right and he should be able to hop with our support.'

They hopped the injured man out to the car and helped him in, then Jess returned with overnight bags. She turned off the lights in the house as she walked to the front door, closing it but not, Clancy noticed, locking it.

If she'd needed anything to remind her she was back in the country, it was that one small detail—unlocked doors.

Mac drove to the airport, this time with Mike loping along behind the vehicle. Clancy helped again to get Rod into the plane, hearing the hissing of his breath as he tried to conquer the pain of his injury while struggling into the back seats.

Jess clambered in after him, seemingly unhampered by her pregnancy, then came Mac, and the little plane taxied away.

Clancy turned to Mike.

'Well, dog, it's just you and me now. Do you suppose if we head back to the house we'll be able to tell which is the drive we follow to the gate?'

Mike smiled his silly smile and Clancy ruffled his head. But it was an absent-minded ruffle, for she was looking up at the massive sky that spread above her and sniffing the fresh, eucalyptus-scented air, and trying very hard to ignore the feeling of well-being that was creeping over her.

'Oh, no, I've done my time in the country and I'm a city girl,' she told Mike. 'Just you remember that!'

CHAPTER THREE

OF COURSE the car wasn't an automatic, but making gear changes must have been burnt into her muscle memory because, with the selection clear from a diagram on the gearstick, Clancy managed three changes with barely a hitch, although once she had it in third she decided to stay there, at least until the end of the drive.

The drive! It went on for ever, forcing Clancy to wonder if she'd somehow chosen the wrong track from the many leading away from the homestead. Although this one had seemed most used, and had trees planted either side, so surely…?

But a front drive four miles long? More, for she hadn't yet reached the gate!

'You're no help,' she said to Mike, who was sitting on the front passenger seat, his head out the window so his long ears streamed back and his lips curled in a kind of grimace.

Clancy drove with her window open as well, so the fresh air rushed through the vehicle.

'The air off the river is fresh,' she told Mike, feeling a need to defend her city living. 'And the South Bank parklands are full of trees.'

But did they diffuse their scent into the air? She had to suppose that if they did, then other city smells—car exhaust and building dust and people perfumes—must mask it.

'Listen to me, Mike!' she snorted, although she hadn't spoken the thoughts out loud. 'Half an hour in the country and I'm being seduced by the scent of it.'

But the scent out here was different from that of the hills around her mother's home. Out here the air was dry and a little dusty, so it carried the perfume of the gum trees easily. Back where she'd grown up, the hills were green, the air moist, the vegetation mostly rainforest with its scent of decaying leaves and mulch.

'Oh, Mike!' she sighed, for no particular reason, then the gate appeared in front of her—not a gate as such but a cattle grid with white-painted fence posts either side.

Turn left, Mac had said, so she turned left, hoping she'd remembered correctly, wondering how far she'd have to go in the wrong direction before some signpost told her she'd made a mistake.

The sun was sinking behind her, so shadows lay across the land on either side of the road, softening the harshness of the landscape, turning the grass a soft blue-green, the leaves on the gum trees lining the road silver in the dimming sunlight.

Peace stole through her, although it was the last thing she should be feeling, alone out here—apart from Mike—with no real idea of where she was going—and, more importantly, why!

Yet peace it was, so she decided to enjoy it, driving along the straight but narrow road, the dog making whiffling noises beside her. This change in the direction of her life was so totally unexpected she could only go with the flow.

'After all, Mike, it's nothing but a diversion—

a little detour on my road through life. The decision was mine.'

Mike turned around so he could lick her cheek, a gesture she took as agreement.

A sharp bark from the agreeable dog brought her out of her little bubble of contentment, and as Mike kept right on barking she slowed the car, pulling off the road onto a flat, grassy verge, listening to engine noises as she did and hearing nothing really bad.

Could a dog know if a vehicle had a flat tyre?

Perhaps he just needed to get out...

But once out, would he get back in?

She looked around the endless plains and shuddered to think of having to find him if he took it into his head to run off.

He was still barking furiously, his head turned back the way they'd come.

'You win,' she said to him. 'There's no way I can drive to town with you making all that noise, so how about we get out and see what happens next?'

She opened the door on Mike's side, not wanting him to leap out onto the road—not that they'd seen another vehicle since they'd left the farm.

Mike set off back along the road, legs lolloping, ears flapping.

Clancy followed more slowly, approaching the spot where Mike had stopped with caution.

The dog was crouched beside another animal, whimpering quietly—another animal that turned out to be a goat.

'Bloody goats!' Clancy muttered to herself, memories of childhood milking duties vivid in her mind.

But as she drew closer she realised the goat was literally bloody, its white and fawn coat black with dried blood.

Kneeling beside it, she murmured quietly, pushing Mike's head out of the way so she could see the injured animal. The soft brown eyes looked trustingly up at her, and she sighed, knowing she had to do something for the animal and praying that something wouldn't be a mercy killing.

She felt the head, free of blood, then down along the spine, coming to the torn skin on the animal's left hindquarters. Something had ripped the skin open and a flap hung loose. The injury was fairly recent, for blood still seeped out of the muscle beneath the tear.

Clancy continued her examination but as far as she could see it was the only injury—although there was a possibility that the left hind leg could be broken.

'I suppose the only thing we can do is take her into town,' she said to Mike, who seemed to agree with this decision as he wagged his tail. 'Is there a vet?'

Mike may have known the answer, but didn't tell her, so Clancy left him guarding his find and returned to the vehicle, pleased to discover some old sacks in the back. She pulled one out, dubious about its cleanliness, but as her overnight bag was in the plane, the sack would have to do.

It wasn't until she tried to put the sack around the injured goat that she realised it was stuck—impaled on the barbed wire of the fence near which it lay.

'It's just one thing after another,' she said to

Mike, trying to hold the animal still while she disentangled the barbs from its pelt. Finally, as the sun sank below the horizon and a hazy dusk settled on the land, the goat was free. She'd brought the car closer and had left the rear door open when she'd got the sack, so now all she had to do was carry the goat over to the vehicle and put it in the back.

Simple!

Except the goat, while not full grown, or maybe of a small breed, was heavier than it looked and getting it into her arms then standing up proved a difficult task.

'You're no help at all,' she told Mike, who frolicked by her side as she struggled with her burden. Eventually the goat was in, Mike was in, and she was ready to continue on her journey.

Before getting behind the wheel, she brushed ineffectually at her clothes, now liberally stained with blood and dirt.

'Your slobber was nothing to the mess I'm in now,' she told Mike.

The town heralded its presence with a tall tower far in the distance.

There followed more towers, but silos this time, evidence of crops being grown in the area. Clancy remembered the sunflowers that had tipped their heads to her in the plane and hoped they grew here too.

'Not that I'm staying,' she reminded Mike. 'But it would be nice to see a field of them close up.'

The town took shape as she drove closer, and she slowed down as she passed the silos and the water tank. Houses began to appear, and ahead what looked like a typical country main street—there'd be a general store, two or three pubs, a motel, one dress shop, one hairdresser, an office housing various government departments—but she should be looking for hospital signs.

Or vet signs?

They were ready for Christmas in Carnock, that much was obvious from the red and green garlands strung across the street, a big golden bell suspended from the middle of each one.

'And light poles festooned with tinsel,' she

said to Mike. 'Carnock gets into Christmas in a big way!'

Mike gave a bark she took to be agreement, or maybe he could read because there was the sign for the hospital.

She swung the lumbering vehicle to the left, up an incline, passing an old two-storeyed brick-and-plaster place that she knew immediately must be Hester's for Mike was whining and looking back towards it.

The hospital—new and modern-looking—spread itself across the top of the hill, trees shading the circular drive in front of it. It, too, was ready for Christmas, with fairy-lights winking and twinkling in the trees and a string of coloured lights around the front entrance.

'You,' she said to Mike, 'will stay in the car.' She wound the windows up to halfway so he wouldn't leap out and join the patients in their beds.

But as she climbed down to ground level, she remembered phoning the hospital—remembered who had answered the phone—and her courage failed her.

As if he understood her need for a little moral support, he gave a short, sharp bark.

Although that might have been a welcoming bark because, tripping down the ramp at the entrance to the hospital, as blonde and beautiful as ever, was Annabelle Crane.

'Clancy,' she called, her voice warm and welcoming, 'I couldn't believe it when Mac said you were on your way. You know, I've been here for six months and somehow never connected you with Hester. Of course, everyone called her Hester so the Clancy part didn't ring any bells in my head.'

She enveloped Clancy in a warm hug, giving an extra squeeze at the end, which indicated to Clancy that Annabelle, too, felt awkward about this reunion.

This was confirmed when her old friend from student days stood back and looked at her.

'Are we okay?' she asked.

Clancy, knowing exactly what she meant, said,

'Of course we are. Stuff happens. And the stuff between us happened long enough ago to be forgotten.'

Did she mean it?

She felt around inside herself and decided she did, and although she would have loved to ask about James and the marriage break-up, Mac had now appeared, charging down the ramp.

'Where have you been?' he roared across the space between them.

Annabelle turned towards him and frowned, then turned back to Clancy.

'Seems you've upset the boss,' she said lightly, but to Clancy it sounded as if Annabelle was pleased Mac was angry, which didn't make sense.

Any more than her flutters did, reappearing as soon as Mac drew near and touched her on the shoulder, as if to reassure himself she was all right.

'Mike found an injured animal. Is there a vet in town?'

'Oh, no, a greenie,' Annabelle declared. 'Re-

ally, Clancy, out here you can't pick up every injured animal.'

'No?' Clancy muttered to herself, following
Mac to the rear door and standing behind him
as he looked at the goat.

'How did you get it in here?' he asked, turning
towards her, his eyes still full of concern.

'Lifted her,' Clancy told him.

Mac grinned at her, and the flutters escalated,
but she was sure now it was the thrill of this detour off her pathway through life that was giving
her these little bursts of excitement.

'Pig!' Mac said.

He turned in time to catch the puzzled frown
on Clancy's face as she said, 'No, it's a goat.'

He smiled at her.

'I do know a goat from a pig, but I'd say she's
been gored by a wild pig. Lucky for her he just
caught the skin, though how she got away from
him I don't know.'

'She was caught in a barbed-wire fence,' Clancy
told him. 'She might have been small enough to
get through it and the pig couldn't.'

'Barbed wire? You untangled her? Come over in the light so I can look at you.'

He took her arm and guided her over to the pool of light at the bottom of the ramp, finding tears in the skin on her fingers, cursing softly to himself, especially as now, beneath the light, he could see just how much blood and dirt had transferred to her clothing.

'Have you had a tetanus shot recently?' he demanded, as a level of concern overtook him.

'Recently enough,' she said, 'and I'll take a look at the scratches when I've had a shower. In the meantime, it's the goat that needs our attention. You didn't answer about the vet.'

'Of course there's not a vet.' Mac hadn't realised Annabelle was still with them until she spoke from behind him. 'And feral goats are in plague proportions out here after all the rain last year. You should have hit it on the head if you wanted to be kind.'

Mac saw the shock on Clancy's face and wondered just how deep her friendship with Annabelle had been—or maybe Annabelle had changed since Clancy had known her. Either way, Clancy had been hurt by the other woman's words and for some reason he didn't like that.

'I'll handle this, Annabelle,' he said, turning to her. 'Would you please check that Rod and Jess are comfortable? See if there's anything they need.'

They stood in silence until Annabelle had disappeared inside the building then Clancy said quietly, 'I don't think it's a feral goat, it was far too docile. It could be some child's pet.'

Mac should have pointed out that the animal had been stuck on barbed wire and also weak from loss of blood, but he didn't, suggesting instead that he'd drive her, Mike and the goat to Hester's house, where he'd leave all three.

'I'll get some anaesthetic and saline to flush the wound, and sutures—whatever I'll need for a bit of goat repair—and come back as soon as I can,' he told her as he drove the short distance to Hester's house.

It was dark, and the house unlit, so it loomed like a great, black shadow against the paler sky.

'Is it friendlier than it looks?' Clancy asked him, and he had to smile.

'Much friendlier,' he assured her. 'Just wait and see.'

He pulled up at the bottom of the front steps and hurried around the car to open her door. He went ahead of her to turn on the lights so the ancient glass shade on the front porch threw a yellow light, and once he was inside and turned lights on there, he knew they'd shed their welcoming glow through the stained-glass panels on either side of the heavy front door.

'Oh, it's beautiful,' Clancy said as she paused in the wood-panelled hallway, looking into the big living room with the comfortable old armchairs facing not a television screen but a big brick fireplace. 'Did Hester sew the quilts?'

Mac looked at the quilts thrown over most of the chairs, not really seeing them for the first time but wondering about them now Clancy had asked.

'I've no idea,' he admitted. 'They've just always been there—there are more on all the beds—but

I don't think I ever saw Hester sewing. Knitting, now, that's another matter, although towards the end her hands were too swollen with arthritis and her eyesight too poor for her to do anything fancy. Somewhere I have a scarf about six feet long that she knitted for me over the last year.'

Clancy had moved across to the old sofa and was examining the quilt laid over it, her hands moving across the faded patterns and colours, her face still.

'I wish I'd known her,' she murmured, then she turned and smiled at Mac.

'I'm not usually sentimental, and I know as well as Annabelle does that it's often kinder to put an animal down than try to save it. It must be the country air affecting me.'

And long may that continue! The thought, popping up out of nowhere, shocked Mac so much he turned away from the smiling woman.

'The kitchen's through here. There's plenty of food in the fridge and pantry—just help yourself. I'll carry the goat around the back—there's a small pen there—and take Rod's vehicle up to the hospital. I should be back within an hour.'

A hint of a frown passed across her face, and he knew he'd spoken too abruptly, but he needed space and time to work out why he kept reacting to this woman the way he did—time to sort out his feelings. Because getting involved with Willow Cloud Clancy was impossible. He'd hurt too many women—not intentionally, but through carelessness and thoughtlessness and inconsideration—and after all Hester had done for him, there was no way he could hurt her great-niece.

Not that she'd shown the slightest interest in him…

Clancy found the kitchen—*and* the dog food. Mike helped her with that by nosing open the pantry door and wagging his tail in front of the big bag of food. His bowls were just outside the back door and she washed them out, filling one with water and the other with dried pellets. The dubious way he regarded his food made her wonder if she'd used the wrong bowls, but when he kept looking from the food to her and back again, she realised that he must have been trained to not eat until he received an order.

But what order?

'Eat!' she told him, but he didn't.

'Okay,' she tried, but that didn't work either.

'Food' was no good so in the end she found the telephone and the useful list of numbers pinned to the wall nearby and phoned the hospital.

Annabelle answered but had no idea of the magic word, although she did tell Clancy that Mac was on his way back.

'Did you just come to see the house or are you staying on for a while?' Annabelle asked, with something more than interest in the question.

'I came to see the house,' Clancy responded, not answering about whether or not she was staying on, because she wasn't sure. Of course, she couldn't stay on for ever, but she could certainly get her lectures prepared out here, and the change might help her put that something extra into them. The something that would inspire her students to be better nurses.

Annabelle, apparently satisfied with Clancy's

answer, said a brief goodbye and hung up. A vehicle was pulling up outside the house—a newer, smaller four-wheel drive. Mac emerged from behind the wheel, a bag in one hand.

'What do I have to say to Mike to make him eat his dinner?' she asked, hoping a sensible question would calm the flutters.

'Did you try "Good boy"?' Mac asked.

She turned away, heading for the back door, where she said the magic words. Mike put his head down and virtually inhaled his dinner, turning to her as the last pellet disappeared with a hopeful look on his face.

'Mac's here now, he can handle you,' she told Mike, while she returned to the kitchen, trying light switches until she found one that lit up the back yard.

It was more of a junkyard than a back yard, she decided, staring out at the clutter of sheds, the piles of old timber and corrugated iron and bricks and stone. But she did see the little pen, one of several, where Mac had left the goat.

Back to the pantry where she found a shallow

dish and a number of clean cloths, some antiseptic and rolls of plaster. Deciding Mac would probably have brought a dressing from the hospital, she put a little antiseptic into the dish, filled it with water and carried it out to the yard.

'I'll clean her up,' she said to Mac, who was approaching from around the side of the house.

Clancy knelt beside the injured animal, sponging away the dirt and dried blood, talking soothingly to it all the time.

Watching her, Mac wondered just what he'd got himself into, going down to Brisbane to find this woman, bringing her back here, disrupting his life in this way.

Although he wasn't to have known she'd cause disruption…

'I think that's it,' she said, standing up so he could see she was still in her soiled clothes, the two animals' welfare more important to her than a shower.

He took her place, aware of her presence beside him as she spread out the contents of his bag while he examined the wound.

'Good to have a trained assistant,' he said. 'Did you get sick of the hands-on work? Is that why you took up lecturing?'

'No!'

Well, that told him. He wanted to probe but the tone she'd used suggested that probing would be useless.

He injected local anaesthetic around the wound, although the lack of response from the goat when he touched her suggested she might be too deep in shock and blood loss to recover. Not that he'd mention that to Clancy.

'She's in a bad way,' Clancy said, and he sighed.

'Pretty bad, but goats are tough. We'll stitch her up then I'll try to get some fluids into her.'

She squatted beside him, passing him what he needed, falling naturally into his rhythm the way all good theatre staff did.

You're stitching a *goat*, he reminded himself— hardly brain surgery.

But it *was* good working with someone who knew what she was doing.

'You'll put in a drip?'

Mac smiled.

'Well, no, I wasn't going to go that far, but I thought I could probably get her to drink some water.'

'A drip might be better,' Clancy said softly, and Mac told himself there was no way he was going back to the hospital to get a drip for a goat.

He stitched quietly, using thick thread, as he knew the animal would try to rub the stitches out as soon as she was on her feet. Clancy must be thinking the same thing, for she snipped each suture close to the skin, and neatened the rough edges of the tear.

The little animal was so quiescent he wondered if their work might be in vain.

Useless to think of a drip—he'd have to immobilise her in some way so she didn't rip it out.

'We could strap her on that old door over there, if you *did* put in a drip.'

Mac turned to look at the woman he had brought into his life.

'Are you always this persistent?' he demanded.

She didn't answer for a moment, looking from

him to the goat. Finally she said, 'More often than not, I was the only child in the commune where my mother lived—where we lived, I suppose—so although I hated having to milk the goats, they became my friends.'

Mac sighed, then stood up, stretching cautiously. It had been a very long day—and was about to get longer.

'Where's this door you're talking about?'

Clancy led him to the door, leaning up against a pile of bricks.

'Bloody junkyard,' he muttered under his breath, then, as his companion turned towards him he explained, 'Hester was always going to get someone in to restore the house, so she collected things she thought might be "useful".'

'I did wonder,' Clancy said, smiling at him as she tilted the door, obviously prepared to help him carry it back to where the goat lay.

Together they secured the goat, Mike supervising the operation.

'I don't suppose, while I go and get some fluid, you could rustle up something to eat? It's a long time since I had lunch and Jess's fruit cake didn't begin to fill the void.'

'Leave it to me,' Clancy declared, smiling so happily that Mac felt guilty that he'd considered *not* providing a drip for the goat.

No involvement, he reminded himself as he drove back to the hospital. Yet that delighted smile lingered in his mind.

Clancy checked the refrigerator. It was easy to see a man had been stocking it—meat, meat and more meat. Well, that didn't worry her. Beer, too, low-alcohol beer, but plenty of it! In the fruit and veggie tray some potatoes, a rather tired-looking lettuce and a tomato, hardly enough to prevent scurvy but it would do for dinner—steak, potato and salad.

First she'd have a quick shower. Although getting into pyjamas would be the sensible thing to do—it had been a long, emotionally exhausting day—she didn't want to walk around in front of Mac in pyjamas that had ladybirds all over them—a gift from her mother last birthday.

Finding the bathroom wasn't easy. She assumed

there'd be one somewhere upstairs but exploring up there without Mac in attendance seemed obtrusive, and being in the country she was fairly certain there'd be a downstairs one somewhere for menfolk returning from the fields.

The first room she peered into was a bedroom, complete with huge four-poster bed, the next a study with a laptop open on the desk—Mac's?—then a library that took her breath away. The walls were lined with shelves, shelves filled with books, even a ladder that moved along the shelves to allow access to uppermost collections. There was a smaller, unused-looking sitting room, a formal dining room with an elaborate but very dusty chandelier and, finally, on the far side veranda, a very basic shower room.

So she grabbed her bag, thankfully left by Mac, showered and dressed—quickly—and returned to the kitchen, finding a grill pan and setting it on the gas stove to heat. She'd microwave the potatoes and put a little butter in them—the refrigerator had told her Mac was a butter man.

Salad—lettuce and tomato would be a bit pathetic. What else could go in the salad?

Further exploration of food stores produced olive oil, olives, feta cheese and some red onions, so all in all the salad wouldn't be too bad.

He returned as she finished mixing it, and she went outside with him to help set up the drip, impressed by his deft movements—and fascinated by the man himself.

The job completed, he went into a room tacked onto the back of the house—one Clancy hadn't noticed in her explorations but which she now took to be a laundry. Then, with water dripping from his hair and beard, he came into the kitchen, grabbing at a towel slung over the back of chair. It seemed he often had a quick wash in the laundry.

'Food?' he said hopefully, and Clancy dropped the steaks onto the now hot grill plate, the sizzle and smell of them prompting a mouth-watering reaction. Suddenly she was starving! She popped the scrubbed potatoes into the microwave and mixed a simple lemon and olive oil dressing, adding a bit of garlic for taste.

'Would you like a drink?' he asked. 'There's beer or beer. Actually, there's probably sherry as well. Hester loved her glass of sherry before dinner.'

He helped himself to a can of beer, and disappeared into the large pantry, returning triumphantly with a bottle of dry sherry and a bottle of red wine tucked under his arm.

'Sherry?'

Clancy shook her head, although she did agree to having a glass of wine with her dinner.

Totally at home in the place, Mac produced a glass for each of them, opening the wine—'to allow it to breathe, as they say'—and setting it on the table. As she turned the steaks he set two places, getting out placemats and coasters for their glasses.

'You're very domesticated,' Clancy teased. 'Do you set up like this even when you're on your own?'

He looked at her, as if startled by her question, then shrugged.

'Two marriages had me fairly well trained, then

Hester rubbed off any rough edges the wives had left behind,' he said, and Clancy knew he wasn't just talking—he was telling her something. Something about himself.

Two marriages?

At thirty-six.

It did seem just a little excessive...

Was he, like her father, another man who 'went away'?

CHAPTER FOUR

MAC saw the expression on Clancy's face and read it as disapproval. Which was good, he decided. Better by far if she was off-side with him right from the start. That way there'd be no complications.

No complications, except that to his body she was like one of the sirens luring sailors onto rocks—magnetically attractive.

Tough!

'Looks and smells delicious,' he said, when she handed him a plate with a still-sizzling steak on it. She smiled her thanks and pushed the salad bowl towards him, then sat opposite him where he'd set her place.

'The food in the pantry,' she asked as she helped herself to salad. 'Was it yours or Hester's?'

'Mostly mine,' he admitted, and Clancy made

a mockery of his conclusion that she disapproved of him by smiling, a warm, natural, just beautiful smile.

'I did wonder if someone of great-aunt status would have balsamic vinegar and olives and feta. Perhaps those stuffed olives that come in bottles, but not big tubs of them.'

Mac found himself returning the smile—impossible not to, really.

'She didn't mind an olive, and she was acquiring a taste for feta, but I couldn't win her over with barbequed haloumi.'

Big mistake, this idle chitchat, for Clancy's smile grew wider and with a teasing glint in her eyes she asked, 'And was one of your wives of Mediterranean descent that you're into such things?'

Wives!

Two disasters!

No more!

But he couldn't snub the smiling woman across the table from him—maybe just keep it light.

'No way. The first was Anglo-Saxon through and through, while the second was Swedish.'

Was he really talking about Kirsten? Mentioning her nationality wasn't talking about her—but he hurried on anyway.

'The olives and feta are my heritage—I'm half-Greek.'

Now her shapely eyebrows rose but the smile still danced around her lips.

'Of course,' she teased, 'I should have guessed. McAlister Warren, a very Greek name.'

He *had* to smile.

'I didn't tell you about the George in the middle of it. For all the string of English monarchs who had the name, George is as Greek as the Acropolis.'

'And the Warren? Was your father or grandfather, called Warrenopoulos and shortened it?'

Mac leaned back in his chair. He had to admit he'd barely scratched the surface of this woman since he'd met her—had it just been this morning?—but the impression he'd got from her flat, her clothes, her conversation was that she was conventional, slightly manic about neatness and also very contained—restrained almost.

Yet here she was, munching on one of the steaks Don the butcher kept especially for him, waving her fork as she spoke and *teasing* him!

Which meant he was in a whole heap of trouble because, for all the physical attraction, if he wasn't attracted to a woman's personality nothing would ever happen between them.

'My mother is of Greek heritage, although she's third-generation Australian,' he explained, when Clancy had finished the mouthful of steak and eaten two olives from her salad—and, no, he hadn't been totally mesmerised by her lips as she'd popped those olives in—and was looking enquiringly at him. 'McAlister was my father's mother's maiden name and my mother, who'd grown up aware of being different, wanted a name for me that was as English—well, Scottish, I suppose—as she could find.'

Clancy studied him for a moment, seeing now the Greek heritage in his near-black eyes and dark good looks.

'Did it bother her?' she asked.

'I think she coped okay. She's beautiful, and it seems to me that unfortunately most people don't care about differences as much when someone is beautiful. On top of which, she's very bright— topped her year in the university law finals— probably topped every year.'

Gorgeous-looking man, beautiful, brilliant mother…

Two wives?

None of your business, Clancy.

'And your father?'

'He's pretty smart as well, State Attorney General at the moment. My parents are both lawyers, which is why I started to study law.'

Clancy tested out the intonation in his words and decided that he liked his father—liked both his parents—for there was deep affection as well as pride in his voice.

'And?' she prompted.

He smiled at her, black eyes aglint again.

'And what?'

'You started law and you've already told me you stopped. Why?'

The glint disappeared.

'Long story that probably wouldn't interest you. Anyway, I'd better finish eating and go and check on your patient.'

But he didn't move, his gaze roving over her instead, so open an appraisal she felt it brush against her skin.

'You've changed clothes—you found your way around upstairs?'

'Found a bathroom out on the side veranda. I didn't like to go upstairs without you here to tell me where to go. I didn't want to end up in your bedroom...'

The words hovered in the air—unconsidered until they'd left her lips. Not that they meant anything, or even hinted at anything, yet rich with suggestion.

Didn't want to end up in your bedroom!

Get past it!

'Or Hester's—anywhere wrong.'

'I'll show you around up there now,' he said,

and although she wanted to protest that she needed to clear the table and wash the dishes— tidy the kitchen—again she read the intonation in his voice and knew he meant that 'now'!

The stairs rose from the right-hand side of the main entrance hall, the railing polished by the hundreds of hands that must have held it through the years. The deep, dark, reddish-tinged wood— she had no idea what kind—was warm beneath her skin.

'Mind this fourth one and the one second from the top,' Mac warned, and Clancy stepped carefully over both, although she did bend to feel each of them—rickety because they'd come loose in the grooves cut into the stringers at the side. Easily enough fixed.

'This big room right at the front is Hester's,' Mac explained, and she forgot about the stairs and listened to his guided tour. 'Well, it was, until she wasn't well enough to climb the stairs. Then she shifted into the downstairs bedroom. Opposite it is the room I'm using, then a bathroom, then another bedroom that I think would suit you as it gets the morning sun but is cool in the afternoon. But it's up to you. There are two more on Hester's side, look at all of them and choose one. There's an en suite bathroom in Hester's room you could use, and another bathroom at the end of this corridor.'

'Four bathrooms in a country house?' Clancy queried.

'I think the little one at the end was for the servants. There are two more bedrooms in the attic. Stairs at the end of this corridor lead up there, but they're steep, so be careful if you go exploring. I don't know if you noticed it from outside, but there's a widow's walk around the attic bedrooms. A small door leads out to it.'

'A widow's walk?'

Mac grinned at her.

'More usually seen near the sea—the narrow railed veranda where the sailors' wives could stand, looking out to sea for the first glimpse of their husbands' ships returning.'

'A widow's walk—I love the sound of it, but it's a reminder of all who didn't return from the sea, which saddens it a bit. But why build a house with a widow's walk out here on the bush?'

Again Mac seemed to study her.

'You really know nothing of your family history, do you?' he asked.

Clancy shook her head.

Mac hesitated for a moment, then said, 'Well, it's too late to go into it all tonight, but tomorrow I'll tell you all about the Clancys.'

The thrill that ran like wildfire through Clancy's blood had to have been fed by the thought of finding her family, not from the flash of Mac's smile as he turned to go downstairs and check the goat.

She followed him more slowly, determined to clean up the kitchen, knowing she wouldn't sleep if the job was left undone.

Fortunately for her peace of mind—and body— there was no sign of Mac in the kitchen, neither did he appear as she washed and dried the dishes then tidied away the placemats and condiments from the table.

Two wives?

She peered through the window above the sink and found she could see the goat, but no Mac.

She wondered if he'd returned to the hospital—as a conscientious doctor or as a man with an interest in Annabelle's sexy laugh.

Not that it was any of her business where he was or what he was doing.

Having a shower, that's what he was doing, she realised when she finally went upstairs to find the bathroom door closed and the sound of water and muffled singing coming from behind it.

She added 'Sings in the shower' to the small store of information she had about her tenant. It went right underneath 'Married twice'.

She'd make the little bathroom at the end of the passage hers so they'd both have privacy, and on that thought she carried her minimal luggage into the room Mac had suggested she take, turned on the light and looked around her in surprise.

The room was like something out of a storybook. Heavy, dark polished wooden furniture, another four-poster bed, flower-garlanded curtains and more flowers on the carpet, the quilt on the big bed also made of flowery patches. Yet nothing clashed, and the whole effect was warm and welcoming, although it had to be tiredness that had Clancy thinking she'd come home.

'You are *not* given to fanciful thoughts!' she told herself, but as she put away her clothes and tucked her overnight bag into the bottom of the heavy wooden wardrobe, the feeling stayed with her, so finally climbing into the bed was like returning to a sanctuary she might have known but not remembered.

'Willow Cloud Clancy, get your head together!' she told herself, speaking the words out loud so they'd have more force.

The night brought dreams—weird dreams! She walked around a widow's walk, peering out to sea, searching for the ship with the skull and crossbones flying on its mast. The wind blew, tangling her long skirts and tugging at long hair, yet for all the clothes and hair she knew the woman who watched and waited was definitely herself.

Something wet was washing over her face. Mist? Waves?

Consciousness began to return. What was it? Where was she?

Forcing herself up through deep layers of sleep, Clancy prised open her eyes, to be immediately confronted by Mike's goofy grin.

'Go away,' she said, not bothering to untuck her arm and give him a push. She closed her eyes and sank back through the layers.

But apparently Mike didn't take rejection lightly, for now he gave a stern yelp.

One eye opened this time.

'Oh, Mike,' Clancy muttered at him. 'Go away and let me sleep.'

'Breakfast!'

Clancy turned her head on the pillow and saw Mac hovering in the doorway, a laden tray in his hands.

'All right if I come in?' he asked, and Clancy glowered at him.

'I don't see why not,' she muttered grumpily. 'Everyone else is in here.'

'Not the goat,' Mac reminded her, setting down the tray on a small table then moving the table close to the bed. 'And don't think this will become a habit. Most days I'm up at the hospital at six, but this morning I figured you must be tired to have slept so well, and surprisingly enough no one killed or injured themselves at the pub last night, so I've had a lazy morning myself.'

'What *is* the time?' Clancy asked him as she reluctantly pushed back the sheet that had been her only covering, and eased her body up against the pillows. The dream lingered in her head—the widow's walk, the pirate ship, the thrill of anticipation she'd felt in her body...

She really needed to head for the bathroom, and she was reluctant to speak when Mac was near in case she had morning dragon breath.

'Nearly ten.'

Mac's reply was so unbelievable she blinked the sleep from her eyes and peered at her watch.

He was right!

'And I can report that the goat is on her feet, off the drip and eating pellet food. Rod and Jess are on their way to Toowoomba where Rod's ankle will be pinned and plated and fixed up good as new. We also have a new arrival in the town, a baby who will go by the unfortunate name of Doofus because that's what his parents called him all the time his mother was pregnant and now they've decided they like it. I suppose we can be thankful it wasn't a girl.'

Clancy blinked again as she battled to take in this stream of increasingly bizarre information, then the need to get to the bathroom overtook any remnants of politeness.

'You're obviously a morning person, I'm not,' she mumbled at him as she clambered out of bed. She did, however, relent to the extent of saying, 'Excuse me,' as she hastened out the door.

The little bathroom she'd decided to claim was further down the passage than she'd remembered, but once there it was good to have a wash and clean her teeth, splash water over her minimal hair and smooth it down, then return to tackle the breakfast.

The image of the pirate ship swirled down the

plughole with the water from her wash, and, clear-headed now, Clancy gave her reflection a little talking to about the difference between fantasy and reality.

'Thank you,' she said, returning to her room to find Mac just outside the door, one hand looped through Mike's collar. 'Are you eating too? I can get dressed quickly and come downstairs.'

He smiled at her, muddling the decision she'd taken about fantasy.

'I ate hours ago. I stayed to prevent Mike sampling your breakfast before you got to it. But I can stay if you like—talk to you while you eat.'

Was he mad? Mac wondered.

When he hadn't been checking the goat's drip, then undoing it when all the fluid had flowed in, *then* standing by at the arrival of Doofus, he had spent the night tossing and turning in his bed, unable to get rid of the image of this woman sleeping just across the passageway.

He'd retained enough common sense to have not clothed her in silky lingerie, but the tiny pair of pyjamas she was wearing, with ladybirds all over them, seemed as sexy to him as any silk or satin night attire.

'Do stay,' Clancy was saying. 'You can tell me about the widow's walk.'

She pulled the curtains to let in the morning light, and settled on a chair beside the table where he'd set the tray, examining the pile of scrambled eggs and pieces of buttered toast.

'This looks delicious. Suddenly I'm starving, so I'll eat and you talk.'

The happy smile she shot him told him just how stupid he'd been to come up here, let alone suggest he stay.

'The widow's walk?' she prompted.

He had to smile. He'd expected questions about Hester, even about her father, but the widow's walk?

He settled into the armchair on the other side of the table.

'Do you know anything about your father's family history?'

She shook her head, finished a mouthful and said, 'Not a thing! And although I think I can remember what he looked like, the man in my memory could be any man who lived with us at some time. He went away—that's all my mother would ever say and now I suspect she didn't know his history either, although it must have been from her I'd heard the name Carnock.'

Mac thought of his parents and his grandparents on both sides. His life had been a living family history lesson, everyone telling him stories of the past. This mattered, he knew, because even when his life had been falling to pieces, when the pain of loss had been at its worst, he'd always known he was part of something bigger and stronger than he was—his family.

'I'll start with the house,' he began, already beguiled by the green eyes that watched and waited for his words. 'It was built by a family called Heathcote who would have been your great-great-great-something grandparents. There's a family tree in the library so you can work out the greats. They had a property out of town—sheep back then—and the property is still there. This was their town house, where they stayed when special events were happening in Carnock.'

'Big house for a weekender,' Clancy observed.

'Big families in those days,' Mac reminded her, watching as she slid a piece of toast with a morsel of egg on it into Mike's slavering mouth. 'And they'd have had a governess for the children, and no doubt a number of maids. I imagine when the farm passed down to the next generation the original family retired here. Anyway, some way back there was a failure in the production line and one lot of Heathcotes had only one child—a daughter named Isabella. In those days women didn't run farms, so she was expected to marry a man who would—but apparently that didn't happen, so the farm was sold and the family moved to this house, with Isabella nursing her ailing parents, who both died fairly young.'

'Leaving Isabella on her own,' Clancy said as brightly as she could, given that she was getting a very creepy feeling about this story.

'Leaving Isabella on her own,' Mac confirmed. He was obviously trying to remember the next bit so Clancy tidied up the tray, ready to take it downstairs. She'd have liked to have changed out of the silly pyjamas, but she couldn't with Mac in the room.

Not that her pyjamas weren't totally decent.

'The story is a bit confused here,' Mac finally continued. 'One tale is that on their last journey from the farm to town the family were held up by a bushranger.'

'Bushrangers in Queensland?' Clancy queried. 'I've never heard of that.'

Mac nodded.

'They were not as well known as some of the ones down south, but we had our share, and the most well known was a chap called McPherson. And, anyway, as I said, it was just a story. The Heathcotes came to town, the parents died and Isabella was living here on her own, which was when she got in touch with one of the carpenters in town and had the widow's walk built around the attic.'

'I can just imagine what the people in a small town made of that!' Clancy said, although inwardly she was cheering for this woman who may or may not have been an ancestor.

'Exactly!'

A smile accompanied the word and it slithered along her nerves.

Diversion—she needed diversion.

'And what happened next?'

'Well, all kinds of stories abound. Isabella kept a horse and often rode out along bush tracks, always alone, although the other young people in the town made up groups to ride to one or other of the waterholes or picnic spots in the mountains.

'Around that time strange things began to happen in the town, ghost stories surfacing. The beat of horse hooves in the night, the jangle of a bridle, the soft neighing of town horses, dogs barking. Strangest of all was that Miss Heathcote was no longer getting schoolboys in to cut the wood for her stove, or help her in the garden, although apparently it took a while for folk to figure that out.'

'The bushranger?' Clancy queried.

'Who knows?' Mac said, teasing her with his grin, 'but what we do know is that some time later an Irishman called Clancy appeared in town. A well-set-up man, not young but not yet old. A good-looking man, a likable man, who, according to the tales, set the hearts of all the young women in a flutter. But it was Isabella he wanted. The town was scandalised. For all he seemed okay, this Clancy was a nobody and Isabella was as close to aristocracy as Carnock had. But it was Isabella he got, scandalising the entire town by marrying her within a month of his arrival, their first child arriving perhaps a little early for the gossips who could count to nine.'

'Good for Isabella! Was she happy, do you know?'

'Hester says yes. Hester vaguely remembered her—Isabella was old, for those days, when she had her first child, so she would have been very old when Hester knew her. She was Hester's great-grandmother so that should help you with how many greats she was for you.'

And she slept in this room, I know she did—

the certainty was firm in Clancy's mind but it was not a thought she could share with Mac...

'A lovely story,' Clancy said instead. Then, deciding practicality was the only way to banish the strange fancies she'd been having, she picked up the tray.

'I'll just take this downstairs and wash the dishes then get dressed and check the goat and explore Mike's domain.' She looked at Mac— she couldn't keep avoiding looking at him. 'Okay with you?'

He nodded.

'Fine, but I'll take the tray,' he said. 'I have to go out for a while but I'll be back for a late lunch. They do a great Sunday lunch at the middle pub if you're interested.'

Sunday lunch at the pub sounded wonderful— but she had to see less of this man, not more. She took a deep breath.

'You don't have to look after me,' she said. 'You've already done more than enough, flying down to Brisbane to find me and bringing me back here, telling me about Isabella.'

He hesitated before answering, then, quite unnecessarily in Clancy's opinion, shrugged his broad shoulders, drawing her attention to his muscled chest and arms.

'I'll still be going to the pub for lunch,' he said. 'Most people do. I'll call by the house in case you want to come along.'

And with that he disappeared in the direction of the stairs.

Well, it's not like it would be a date, Clancy told herself. 'I'll call by in case you want to come along' was hardly a pressing invitation, but she riffled through the small collection of clothes she'd brought with her, and wished she'd thought to pack something bright—a skirt maybe.

Although as far as she could remember, she didn't own a skirt. A couple of dresses for formal occasions, and slacks, capris, shorts, shirts and T-shirts made up her entire wardrobe.

For a moment she felt nostalgia for the clothes she'd worn when she'd been young—the bright, tie-dyed, Indian-cotton shifts, and long sweeping skirts in vivid green or purple. Had it been rebellion against all that colour that she'd settled into white and navy, with an occasional bold excursion into cream or black?

Looking around the flowery bower of a bedroom, she smiled to herself. Being a woman of her time, for all she'd married a bushranger, Isabella's clothes would have been subdued in colour—practical dark colours—which might be why she'd thrown caution to the winds in her bedroom and furnished it with flowers.

What *was* she thinking? She didn't even know it was Isabella's room, and for all she knew it could have been redecorated ten times over since Isabella had lived in the house.

Clancy dressed—navy shorts and blue and white striped shirt—then went down to visit the goat.

It was standing at the back door, having somehow got out of the pen—not entirely unlikely given the state the pen was in. But it hadn't taken off, seemingly content to be around a house, strengthening Clancy's notion that it had been a pet.

'You want food?' she asked it, then realised any food in the house would belong to Mac so she could hardly start feeding it to a goat. 'Eat grass until I get back from the shops,' she told it, wondering if Carnock would have a green-grocer—and if it did, whether it would be open on a Sunday. Someone else probably took left-over fruit and vegetables but it would be worth-while finding out.

She cut off the thought, appalled that her mind seemed to be considering her stay in Carnock as a long-term arrangement, for herself as well as the goat...

Staring out over the mess in the back yard, towards gum trees lining the small river, she couldn't help but think back to her little apart-ment. Yes, it was convenient, and neat, and had suited her situation, but how empty compared to all she saw around her now, how characterless, how unappealing—how dull!

She pulled on the floppy cloth hat she'd brought with her, picked up her handbag and headed down the road, mentally charting her way to the main part of the town. Hospital up there on the hill, so down the hill then turn left—that was the main road she'd come in on, and if the town was true to form, the main road would lead her to the shops.

Sunday—would country-town shops be open on a Sunday?

After a long walk she discovered one was—a supermarket that had obviously been built by putting two or three smaller shops together, modernising the ground floor of an old brick building. Mindful of a fair walk back in the hot sun, she bought milk and cereal and bread, then lettuce, carrots and a bag of apples for the goat.

She'd have to talk to Mac about the goat, and, if she was staying for longer than a couple of days, about contributing to the food supplies in the house.

Walking back, she couldn't help but think of Isabella. She'd have had a basket over her arm, not a number of green 'Save the Planet' bags. Maybe her Irishman had shopped with her, carrying the basket home.

'Hey, don't go lugging all that stuff around on a hot day. You should have told me what you needed. Hop in.'

Not a bushranging Irishman, but a Greek-Australian. Mac pulled up beside her, chastising her still as he took the bags from her and thrust them into his car.

'I thought you had business out of town this morning,' she reminded him.

'So did I,' he said, which didn't make much sense, although the way he said it suggested he'd have preferred to be anywhere but here.

Why?

He didn't seem like a man who'd resent any interruption to an ordered lifestyle—far too laid-back—and really, being a doctor, especially a country doctor, he could hardly expect an ordered lifestyle.

One way to find out…

'Do you mind me being here? Is it a nuisance for you?'

She watched him as she asked the question, seeing him in profile, his face dark against the lightness of the sky outside the window. Saw him frown, then begin to speak, but close his lips again before a word was uttered.

Finally, when she'd decided he was going to ignore the question, he answered her.

'No!'

Just no?

That was it?

They pulled up at the side of the house, but before he could get out—escape?—she asked, 'No, you don't mind me being here or, no, it isn't a nuisance?'

He turned now to look at her and although she expected at least the shadow of a smile, his face was serious.

'I doubt you'd ever be a nuisance,' he said, then he opened his door, slid out, retrieved her bags and stalked towards the house, around the back, suggesting this was his usual way in.

Clancy followed more slowly, stopping just inside the back-yard gate to scratch the goat's head and fondle her silky ears.

'You need a name,' she told the animal. 'You look like a Dolly. Would you like that for a name?'

Mike came bounding out from somewhere, which meant when she finally went into the kitchen, her green bags were on the table but there was no sign of Mac.

He'd intended driving out to Heathcote to have a chat with his manager there, but Mac had no sooner left town than a mad urge to return had overtaken him.

Not so much a mad urge to return to the house, but a mad urge to spend more time with Clancy.

Given his situation and his determination not to get involved with her, it was totally irrational, but he'd turned the car around, delayed things just a little by calling at the pub to book a table for two for lunch, then felt a sudden leap in his chest when he'd spotted her labouring back up the road with her shopping bags.

The leap had confirmed he'd done the wrong thing, but by then it had been too late.

Now sitting in the study, staring at a blank computer screen, he tried to analyse his behaviour.

Apart from her name, Willow Cloud Clancy was about as ordinary as you could get. A neat, self-contained woman leading an orderly life, and while, yes, she had spectacular eyes, and skin like the bloom of a tropical peach, she just wasn't his type. And even if she was, he wasn't going to get involved with her.

Of course he could argue he was only doing his duty to Hester, who had been his prop and guiding light when he had been going through the aftermath of Kirsten's death, but being attracted to Clancy wasn't part of that duty.

Was it prolonged celibacy that had thrown his libido into overdrive when he'd met Hester's great-niece?

No, if it had been that, he'd have taken up Annabelle's open invitation to a 'no strings' affair.

Could still, if it came to that!

Annabelle—could he talk to her about Clancy, unobtrusively of course? Maybe learning more

about her would be enough to cool the unexpected ardour.

He rested his elbows on the desk and sank his
head into his hands, ruffling his over-long hair,
feeling the beard shadow on his cheeks, thinking he needed a haircut and a shave—wondering
where he'd come across such a word as 'ardour'.

Was that even a word?

Did it mean what it sounded like?

Attraction with a hint of lovesickness…

He groaned and reminded himself that Aussie
men didn't do lovesickness, any more than Greek
men did. Spaniards maybe, Italians, definitely,
but Aussie men—Greek-Aussie men?

What a laugh!

CHAPTER FIVE

THE phone call shattered his moody deliberations.

'Kate at the hospital, Mac. The Rogerses have just brought Jack in. He complained of a headache and nausea then kind of passed out.'

'I'll be right there. Just ask them what he's been doing lately—out drinking last night, any sport over the last few days, food he's eaten, etcetera. Tell them I'm on my way.'

He bumped into Clancy as he left the room.

'Problem?' she said, picking up on his haste.

'Teenage kid, disoriented, nauseous, then passed out.'

'Drugs?' Clancy asked as she followed him down the hall to the front door.

Mac shrugged.

'Unlikely, knowing Jack, but he's a teenager so it could be anything.'

'Can I come with you? Have a look around the hospital? Maybe talk to Annabelle.'

He should be seeing less of her, not more, but then he wouldn't really be 'seeing' her at the hospital. Although he couldn't fool himself he wouldn't be aware of her presence somewhere in the building.

'No worries,' he heard himself say.

They walked out to the car, Mac pleased to find that for all the confusion in his body, he still had the ability to focus totally on what lay ahead. Young Jack? What had the town's best athlete and undoubted wild child been up to lately?

In fact, he was so focussed be barely noticed Clancy's presence in the car, apart from picking up on a faint, citrusy perfume.

'What do you know?' Clancy asked, helping him to stay on track.

'Only that he was feeling ill and is now unconscious.'

He pulled up at the hospital where Kate and Jack's father had already lifted the lad onto a wheeled stretcher and pushed him into the big, and surprisingly empty, emergency room.

'He was playing cricket last weekend and got hit on the head with a bouncer,' Greg Rogers explained as Mac examined the unconscious teenager. 'But he's been okay since then. I kept asking about headaches—so I don't see how it can be that. Then just at lunchtime he felt sick, and now this.'

The fear in Greg's voice reached into Mac and tightened like a fist around his gut. Head knock, haematoma, but chronic, slow to show itself, not acute.

Or drugs?

He turned to Kate.

'Who's on duty?'

'Just me,' the cheerful enrolled nurse responded. 'No patients so Annabelle went down to Toowoomba with Jess and Rod yesterday.'

Great. Except he had someone else here. A theatre nurse, trained and experienced enough to lecture on the subject.

He slid the phials of blood he'd been taking

into a kidney dish. Kate could manage the basic tests for common drugs, simple tests they could do at the hospital.

'You do these and ask Clancy to come in. Woman with short hair, she's having a look around the hospital so she shouldn't be hard to find. I'll take Jack through for a CT scan—tell her where I'll be.'

He turned to Greg.

'Don't worry, he'll be okay. I just need to check things out and then I'll tell you what comes next. There's a new coffee machine in the waiting room—help yourself and relax as much as you can.'

Greg looked at his son, watching until Mac wheeled him out of sight. Mac felt a moment of gladness that he had no children—he was spared the pain he could read on Greg's face and in the white-knuckled fists he held stiffly by his sides.

'Hit on the head by a cricket ball last weekend,' Mac said to Clancy as she came in. 'If it is a sub-dural haematoma that's grown large enough to cause unconsciousness, I'll have to drain it now.

I can't afford to send him somewhere else—it could be too late when he gets there.'

He set up the machine and with Clancy's help lifted Jack onto the table while he was explaining, adding, as they moved away and Jack's body slid into the cylinder, 'Annabelle's not here. I've no experienced staff so would you help?'

'Of course, but do you do much surgery here? Do you have a lot of surgical equipment?'

Mac didn't answer, his attention on the screen.

'See here,' he said. 'Left-sided subdural haematoma, see the slight midline shift of the ventricles.'

He was talking to himself, really, making sure he had the picture clear in his mind, although he'd have it up in Theatre as well.

'I don't do much surgery,' he admitted, finally answering her question. 'I do simple things, but we also have the flying surgeon come in every couple of months so, yes, the theatre is well stocked. When the surgeon comes I act as his assistant, so I'm not a novice.'

Jack slid out of the machine and they shifted

him back to the trolley, Mac guiding it as they rolled him to Theatre, Clancy trying to remember what she knew about subdural haematomas.

'Three classifications, aren't there?' she said to Mac. 'Acute, sub-acute and chronic.'

'Acute usually develops immediately after the injury, and the mass of blood caught in the dura matter of the skull is very dense. It almost always requires a craniotomy.'

'Opening up a square of the skull so the surgeon can take out the clot and repair the blood vessels?' Clancy queried.

They'd reached the theatre, but before pushing Jack through the doors, Mac nodded and finished what he was saying. It helped him sort out the thoughts pinging around in his head.

'Sub-acute develops in two to fourteen days—which fits with this—and chronic is also slow to show itself. I don't think we need to classify it down to either one, we just need to get to it.'

They rolled Jack into Theatre.

'Chronic and sub-acute can be drained through a burr hole—two if necessary. We can do that here to relieve the pressure on the brain, then send him on to a specialist who can incorporate the burr holes into a craniotomy if he needs to do one.'

They lifted Jack onto the operating table as Mac was talking, Clancy looking at the pale young face surrounded by a mop of blond, curly hair and praying he'd be all right.

'Tell me where to shave and I'll do that and prep him while you get what you need.'

'Dilantin first, to prevent any seizures. Then I'll put a catheter into his hand for the anaesthetic and later he'll need fluids to help the brain re-expand.'

Mac was talking to himself, Clancy realised, but he moved quietly and efficiently, first inject-ing the Dilantin, then an anaesthetic, before set-ting what he wanted on a surgical trolley.

'Gloves in that cabinet and gowns, caps and aprons in the cupboard through that door,' he said.

'What about this hair?' Clancy asked him, aware they needed to be as quick as they could, and worried if she left the long hair close to the wound it would increase the risk of infection.

'Take off an area about ten centimetres square and tie up the rest if you can, keeping it back from that area. We've no time to cut it all off and anyway he might object to that. Put a cap on him for now, and he can decide for himself if he wants the lot shaved when we've got him back with us. Now, I need to talk to his father. You okay?'

He looked at her and smiled, and although his concern for his patient and what lay ahead was written clearly on his face, the smile was still good enough to warm her in ways it shouldn't.

Clancy cut the long locks and shaved the skin over the area Mac had indicated. She slathered the skin with antiseptic and stepped out of the way, finding a gown, scrubbing her hands and pulling on gloves, awkward on her own, before checking the equipment Mac had on the trolley. The drill was small, like a tool you'd see in a workshop.

A small thrill ran through her. Was it being

back in a theatre? Or working with the man who'd brought her to this place?

Mac returned, already gowned, frowning now. She realised just how concerned he must be— if he didn't release the pressure in Jack's brain, the teenager could end up with brain damage, or die. Mac scrubbed and gloved again before approaching the operating table.

'It should be right here,' he muttered, and began cutting the skin, releasing a flap he could peel back to allow access to the skull and staple into place across the burr hole later.

Clancy passed instruments to him, remembering the pleasure of teamwork in operating theatres. In most hospital work, come to that.

'Do you miss this work?' Mac asked, and although she knew he was talking, like many surgeons did, to ease his own tension, she was surprised he should have tuned into her thoughts.

'Now I'm here I realise I do,' she said, as he carefully separated the skin from the bony skull. 'But I enjoy lecturing as well, especially when I have students who are excited about their future and really want to be nurses.'

'As against those who are taking the course because it seemed like a good idea at the time or they got the right marks to get into it?'

Clancy smiled and nodded, although all Mac's attention was now on the tiny hole he was drilling into Jack's skull.

Blood oozed out, showing the drill was through to the protective linings of the brain. Mac set down the drill and she passed him a suction device so he could excavate as much of the clot as possible, their gloved fingers touching.

'I'll leave in the small drain,' he said, and she unwrapped the sterile wrapping from the fine, soft tube and passed it to Mac. 'Now I'll staple up the flap and we'll keep him an hour or so before we send him down to Toowoomba to see a specialist. Chances are he'll be okay, but down there they can do an MRI and if there's another bleed or residual clotting, there'll be have a specialist on hand to fix it. Right now, he needs to lie flat, with fluid running into him.'

He finished his stitching, set a dressing over the wound, then walked away, stripping off his gloves.

'Do you mind staying here with him for a little while? I need to speak to his father.'

'I'm happy to stay,' she said, although when Mac walked out the door she breathed a sigh of what could only be relief. Working with him had been peculiar, to say the least. For a while there it had seemed as if they'd always worked together, which was stupid, and probably a hangover from when she'd worked in Theatre with James.

Then there was last night's weird dream of Isabella on the widow's walk. Could dry outback air make you fanciful?

Desperate to recapture her calm, sensible self, she cleared the trolley, finding the right bins for the refuse, and another container for surgical instruments that must be sent away for sterilisation.

Mac returned with Greg Rogers, introducing him to Clancy.

Greg shook her hand and thanked her for her

help, then asked, 'Mac says you're Hester's great-niece?'

'Apparently,' Clancy replied, wondering just how long it would take for news of her arrival and relationships to get around the small town.

'Then you must be Robert's daughter?'

Her mother had called him Robbie so she'd never thought of her father as a Robert. Robert seemed such a responsible name.

Clancy nodded.

'Well, that's great. I went to school with him—where's the old bugger now and what's he up to? He went away and no one ever heard another word of him. Not even Hester, who'd brought him up when his mum and dad were killed in that accident.' He paused, then added, 'But you'd know all that.'

Not wanting to admit she didn't know all that, and more than a little shocked by the information—how old had her father been when his parents died and how had their deaths affected him? And was it because of that trauma in his youth he'd become a man who 'went away'?

'I don't know where he is,' she said. 'He went away when I was quite young.'

'Oh, I am sorry,' Greg replied, and he reached out and squeezed her shoulder. 'But he was a great bloke,' he assured her, though not very forcefully as it obviously occurred to him that maybe a man who went off and left a child might not be so great.

'I've phoned for the ambulance to take Jack down to Toowoomba.' Mac had been watching Clancy's face during Greg's reminiscences and decided it was time to cut them off. 'As I told you earlier, Greg, this is purely precautionary. It's best he gets a complete check from a specialist down there. Will Beth want to travel with him? Or you? Or you could both drive down.'

'Beth'll want to go in the ambulance. I'll pop outside and give her a call—I've already told her what you've done and that he's going down to town. She can chuck some clothes for all of us into a bag and I'll pick her up and bring her back here to the hospital.'

He hurried off, but turned at the door to address Clancy.

'Now, don't forget, I owe you one, so if you want to know anything about your dad's early years, see some photos perhaps, just pop in any time. The hardware store—that's mine. Me and Beth both work there—Jack too.'

His attention had shifted to his son at the end of the sentence and his voice quivered.

'Thanks,' Clancy said, 'and don't worry about Jack. He'll be fine.'

He hurried away.

'Are you?' Mac asked when Greg had departed. Clancy looked puzzled. 'Fine?' he added, then as she still seemed bewildered said, 'Are you okay?'

She smiled at him, the cheeky gamine grin that caused such problems in his chest.

'Mac,' she said, looking him firmly in the eye, 'I am not going to fall apart every time I meet someone who knew my father. After all, didn't you tempt me to come here with words about family history and roots and learning about my father? No, now I want to know more, not less, and more about Hester as well, about all my ancestors.'

She didn't mention Isabella, although she was the one who burned in Clancy's mind, the bare bones of the story Mac had told her resonating with her in some strange way.

'That's good,' Mac said, and touched her lightly on the shoulder—the touch of a colleague, nothing more, but it did distract Clancy from her thoughts of Isabella.

The ambulance arrived and they saw Jack safely into it, the papers detailing his treatment passed to one of the attendants. A woman, obviously his mother, arrived and clambered in the back with one attendant and her son, while Greg stood a little apart, watching until the vehicle drew away.

'Kids!' he said, and hearing the anguish in his voice Clancy went to him and put her hand on his arm.

'He's going to be fine. Stop worrying about him and concentrate on getting yourself to

Toowoomba safely. Both he and your wife are going to need your support down there.'

Greg smiled at her, and ruffled her hair with his hand.

'Rob's kid, eh, telling me what to do. Your dad was the same—always bossy!'

He gave her a quick hug, put out his hand to Mac, said, 'You're right, I'll be careful,' and climbed into his big dual-cab ute.

Clancy stood with Mac as he drove away, watching until he'd disappeared from sight. Then, to Clancy's surprise, Mac put *his* arm around her shoulders and *he* gave her a hug.

'And what's that for?' she asked—well, demanded, really—because the hug had started more than flutters in her body and her reaction bothered her. 'I told you I was fine.'

Mac studied her before replying, a smile almost coming through.

'Well,' he drawled, 'I figured if a total stranger could give you a hug without getting his face slapped, I might give it a go.'

She had to laugh, and her laughter sorted out the flutters...kind of.

'Three-thirty. A bit late for lunch at the pub, but we can still go down and see if they've any leftovers.' Mac had moved away from her, and was looking over her shoulder as he spoke, so she had to wonder if he felt obliged to feed her when he had something better to do.

Besides, did she *want* to have lunch at the pub with Mac?

Yes, her body answered. Not really, said her head, although if they had lunch at the pub he might tell her more about Isabella and the Irishman.

Was that really her head talking, or her body looking for excuses to be with him?

'Okay,' she muttered when she realised he was waiting for a reply.

'Well, don't overwhelm me with enthusiasm,' he teased, but the sparkle had gone from his eyes, replaced with what looked like wariness.

Was he as ambivalent as she was over this lunch?

Too bad if he was. Now she'd decided to go, she was going.

They walked together out to the car, the silence not awkward but too conducive to wayward thoughts.

Physical thoughts.

'Did you choose Carnock or did it choose you?' she asked Mac, and as the words came out she realised it wasn't just an idle question but that she *did* want to know.

'I switched from law to medicine so I could become Carnock's doctor.'

'You did *what*?' Clancy asked, the words not making any sense.

Mac answered with a smile, but it wasn't one of his best efforts, and his eyes certainly weren't twinkling. If anything, they were looking back into the past.

'I spent most of my school holidays here, staying with my grandparents, my mother's parents. You must know that in the early days every country town in Queensland had a Greek café, usually called the Star or the Acropolis. My great-great-grandfather established his café right here in Carnock, probably at about the time your Isabella was moving into town. Why or how he came to choose Carnock is lost in the mists of time, but he established the Athina, named after his mother, and the business flourished.'

Mac opened the door of the car for her and she ducked past him to get in, being careful not to brush against him lest an accidental touch made this togetherness more difficult than it already was.

'And your great-grandfather carried it on?' she asked as he slid behind the wheel and drove carefully out of the hospital grounds, his gaze fixed on the road ahead.

'He did, indeed,' he said eventually, although she could hear tension in his voice. 'He expanded his empire to build a picture theatre next door to the café—one of those outdoor ones they had in the country—a screen and canvas chairs.'

'Outdoors?'

'It was all the rage at the time, although it worked better in places like Western Australia where there was less chance of rain. The screen end had cover because that's where the piano was as well—I'm talking silent-movie days.'

Clancy shook her head, though she was pleased to hear the enthusiasm and, yes, affection back in Mac's voice.

'I wish I'd seen it,' she said. 'I simply can't imagine it—but how wonderful it must have been for the people of the time to be able to sit under the stars and watch a story unfolding in front of them.'

'Exactly!' Mac said, pulling up in front of what Clancy realised must be the 'middle' pub.

'Oh, what a great old building!'

She stared at the two-storey structure with its green and cream Federation paintwork and the iron lace adorning the veranda that ran around the upper storey.

'This,' said Mac with not a little bit of pride in his voice, 'was my grandfather's pride and joy. His father had started the building but it was my grandfather who made it what you see today, although the upkeep is enormous with the paintwork and the stained glass in all the ground-floor windows.'

'Was it affected by the flood?'

'Don't talk about it!' Mac groaned. 'We got most of the stuff up to the upper floor but the beer barrels are kept in the cellar and pipes from there to the bars all filled with floodwater. The locals had to drink bottled beer, and warm beer at that, because the power to all the cool rooms was cut off. Come inside, I'll show you the mark on the bar where the floodwaters peaked.'

He led her across a wide veranda and through one of the open French doors into a bar where people, men and women, called greetings to him.

Acknowledging them with a nod or a wave, he took Clancy to the bar and pointed out the mark with the date of January's floods.

'The other marks?' she asked.

'Previous floods,' Mac explained, showing the dates, one thirty years earlier, one ninety.

'It looks as if it doesn't happen too often,' she said, and his heartfelt 'I do hope not' told her that the pub must still be in his family.

But he was on the move again, leading the way out of the bar, across the hall that led to the front door, past a massive old wooden staircase and into what must be the dining room.

'I know we're late, Nellie, but is there any chance of food?'

He spoke to a woman who was laying table for the next meal—presumably dinner that night.

'Heard about young Jack and kept you a meal,' she said, then she switched her attention to Clancy. 'So, you're Rob's girl,' she said, not actually smiling but without any animosity. 'You could have had a heap of siblings in this town only he was a careful one, that Rob.'

She whisked away, leaving Clancy to ponder what had happened.

'Was Nellie saying what it sounded like?' she finally asked Mac. 'That she'd been one of my father's girlfriends at one time?'

Mac's grin was back and as she caught it, sparks of fire slid down her belly, homing in on that sensitive place between her thighs.

'Ask her yourself. I'll introduce you properly when she comes back.'

Nellie returned within minutes, plates loaded with roast pork and baked vegetables.

'Oh!'

She hadn't meant it to, but the sound came out as a moan, Clancy's hunger making itself felt as her mouth watered at the delicious smells.

'And crackling,' she said, poking the crispy golden skin with her fork. She looked up at Nellie. 'Thank you so much! This looks delicious. Living on my own, I never cook a roast. I'm Clancy, but you know that.'

She held out her hand, although all she really wanted to do was get stuck into the meal in front of her.

Nellie shook her hand.

'Welcome to Carnock,' she said. 'I think you'll like it here, and I know everyone will make you welcome. Everyone loved Hester and most everyone loved Rob.'

For a moment Clancy considered telling her she wasn't staying, but then...

'Thank you,' she said, and was glad when Nellie departed, pausing long enough at the door to tell them there was more if they wanted it.

Mac looked at the woman he'd brought into his life, wondering how she'd wormed the story of his ancestors out of him without even trying. Wormed her way into his consciousness.

She was fully focussed on the food in front of her, but he had to wonder why she hadn't told Nellie she wasn't staying.

And she wasn't staying—because what did Carnock hold for her?

A house and a dog—arrangements could be made for both. He'd be happy enough to stay on in the old house if that's what Clancy wanted. He and Mike were used to each other and the legal issues could be sorted.

'This is fantastic!'

Clancy looked up from her plate for long enough to share this observation.

'You're not eating,' she added.

'I will,' he said. 'I was enjoying watching you enjoy it.'

She glanced his way again, the quick smile lighting up her face.

'Being a pig, you mean. But, honestly, I rarely cook for myself and never food like this. I might throw a sausage in a frying pan, or some other piece of meat.' The smile broadened. 'Meat didn't figure largely in my childhood and now I'm addicted to it.'

She kept throwing him scraps of information about her childhood, not enough for him to put a complete picture together, just odds and ends that tantalised him. He knew enough about the hippie communes that had grown up around Nimbin in the nineteen-sixties to imagine some of it, but only some.

He tackled his lunch, wondering about her, wondering why he was so curious...

'So, your grandfather made the pub what it is today.'

Her immediate hunger assuaged, Clancy broke the silence that had fallen between them.

'Is he still alive? Is it still in the family?

Mac looked up at her, again no twinkle in his eyes.

'No to the first question and yes to the second. It's mine.'

She knew she was frowning but it didn't make sense.

'What's yours?'

Now he smiled but still no twinkle.

'The pub, of course. My mother owns the café, although it's had a manager running it for years, but my grandfather didn't think a woman should own a pub, so it came to me. That and the property my grandfather bought when he decided he was Australian enough to be a farmer and not a café proprietor. Mum didn't want the property and it would have been mine eventually.'

It seemed to Clancy that the flow of information stopped rather abruptly, and she felt a twinge of disappointment because as well as enjoying learning more about this man, she loved listening to his voice.

Never mind, there was another piece of crackling that had been hiding under the apple sauce, and she concentrated on eating that without crunching *too* loudly.

Then, out of the blue, the rich, chocolate voice came again.

'The property is Heathcote.'

'Nice name,' Clancy said, through a mouthful of half-crunched crackling.

'It means nothing to you?' Mac probed.

She swallowed, trying to think, aware from Mac's question that it should. Perhaps it was being in his company that made her brain slow to work—the stupid organ too busy processing little things she kept noticing about him, like the way his long fingers rested easily on the cutlery...

'Should it?' she said, dragging herself back into the conversation.

'Heathcote? Isabella Heathcote?'

His dark eyes were watching her closely so they probably picked up on the little shiver that ran through her body as the coincidence of it all loomed like some inevitable fate.

'You own Isabella's old home? Her family property?'

'*Your* family's property,' Mac said, and Clancy told herself she had to ignore shivers like she had to ignore sparks and flutters, and definitely had to forget any idea of inevitable fates.

'Well, it's been long gone from the family,' she said, pretending to an ease she was far from feeling. 'Is the house in better condition than the one in town?'

And before he could answer, another thought flashed into her mind, a practical thought, one that would certainly divert her from fates, inevitable or otherwise.

'Oh,' she said, 'that's what I wanted to do this afternoon. Fix those two wobbly stairs.'

And with a plan in place for what was left of the afternoon, she tackled the rest of her lunch, only slightly diverted when Mac said, in a faint voice, 'Fix the wobbly stairs?'

Assuming it was a rhetorical question, she kept eating...

CHAPTER SIX

'I'll drop you back at the house and go on to the hospital,' Mac said as they left the pub.

His guest—or, if truth be told, his hostess—turned to face him.

'But there are no patients in the hospital—I looked through it before Kate called me in to help in Theatre.'

Green eyes, clear skin—surely there had to be more to attraction than that!

Focus!

'Ah, but you didn't look further than the main building. Out the back there's what we call "The Annex". It's not exactly a nursing home, more a hospice, although not really that either. The men and women living there need more care than they'd get in a nursing home and, yes, some of them haven't long to live, but some of them are quite healthy.'

'Dementia?'

Mac nodded.

'Two, and one with Parkinson's that's almost reached end stage, a treasure who is one hundred and three and believes maybe one hundred and twenty would be a good age to move on, an older man who has had unstable diabetes all his adult life and has lost his lower limbs above the knee, and—'

He stopped, not wanting to talk about Helen, but even though he'd only known Clancy a little over twenty-four hours, he should have known she wouldn't let him get away with an unfinished sentence.

'And?' she prompted, right on cue.

'I'm going up to see Helen Lawrence, diagnosed four years ago with MND.'

'Motor neurone disease.' Clancy barely breathed the words. 'Four years ago? She's done well, but—'

He heard the depth of Clancy's understanding in that 'but', and felt her empathy.

'She has family here?'

Mac nodded.

'Three kids, two younger boys and a daughter, Allysha, who is fifteen.'

'Old enough to know her mother's going to die. And what a terrible thing, that knowing.'

To Mac's surprise tears had welled in Clancy's eyes and her voice was gruff with emotion, then she sniffed defiantly and grinned at him.

'For all she's truly off the planet about some things, my mother is so wonderful I cannot imagine life without her somewhere in the universe. And at fifteen? I could have gone completely off the rails—any young girl could.'

Obviously embarrassed by her show of emotion, Clancy strode across to the car and climbed in. Mac followed more slowly, wondering if he'd ever known anyone as easy to talk to as Clancy was.

'That's Helen's fear for Allysha,' he said when he joined her in the car. 'She can't verbalise it but I can read it in her eyes. The school's not big enough to have a counsellor, and although I've arranged for one to visit from time to time, Allysha hasn't opened up to anyone. She has two younger brothers and she mothers them. If I try to probe she says she's far too busy keeping them in line to be bothered with stuff like inner feelings.'

'You need Hester back,' Clancy said, and Mac stared at her in surprise.

'I've thought that a hundred times. Unfortunately, by the time we realised how badly Helen was deteriorating, Hester wasn't well enough for me to be thrusting my problems on her.'

'And Helen's husband?'

'He's good with the kids and keeps the house going, but he's devastated by what's happening and he's going to crash and burn before too long. He's an excellent mechanic and was working in the mines before this happened, FIFO.'

'FIFO?'

Mac smiled at her.

'Fly in fly out—it's a common term these days. All kinds of tradesmen and labourers work in the mines on a two-weeks-on, one-week-off rotation. He's been flying in to a mine in the northwest from Toowoomba but with the kids on school holidays he feels he has to be at home with them. The company is good, but they can't be expected to pay him if he's not working, and he's trying to build up as big a bank balance as he can so the kids have financial security if something happens to him.'

'Why don't Allysha and the boys come and stay with us?'

The idea had seemed so obvious to Clancy she was surprised when Mac stopped the car, slap bang in the middle of the road. Thankfully no one was out and about in Carnock this late Sunday afternoon.

'Come and stay with *us*?' Mac repeated in a stunned voice.

'Us, you and me, in Hester's house,' Clancy elaborated as the idea took root in her mind. 'There's a ton of room, all that gear in the back yard for the boys to build cubbies, there's Mike and the goat to take their mind off things, and they can help me with any jobs I decide to do—like fixing the stairs.

'And if I'm around the place and Allysha's there as well, she might just decide to talk to me. And even if she doesn't, I can take a little bit of the responsibility for the boys off her shoulders. They can still go home to their dad when he's in town, just shift between the two houses.'

The blast of a car horn told them there was at least one other car out in town today and Mac reacted, moving forward, but slowly, as if caught up in a dream—or maybe a nightmare.

'You don't mind kids, do you?' Clancy asked. 'I mean, you seem to get on with Mike, and kids aren't that different from dogs—feed them, water them and show your affection, those are the main things.'

'But you don't even know these children,' he protested, and Clancy laughed.

'Trust me,' she said. 'Kids are kids. I earned my "going away to uni" money babysitting, and kept myself through college with nannying. I might not be as good as that rather fearsome nanny on TV, but I'm more than competent.'

Mac sighed, and said, 'Of course you are,' in a faint voice, finally pulling into the drive at Hester's house. 'Look, I'll ask Helen and see her reaction and we'll talk about it later.'

'I should go up and meet her myself. She certainly won't want to hand her kids over to me without looking me over. The way you talk, she's still okay mentally.'

Another sigh.

'Sometimes I think that's the hardest part, the fact that she knows how quickly she's deteriorating and the frustration of not being able to reveal how she feels about it.'

'Poor woman,' Clancy said, 'but at least if she gives the okay to this idea, it will be one less thing for her to worry about.'

She opened the car door, but didn't get out, turning to Mac instead.

'Should I come up with you now?'

Mac was studying her with a peculiar intensity.

'What?' she demanded, and he shook his head

for the third time. At this rate it would probably drop right off after a week or two...

'You know,' he said, slowly and carefully, 'I walked into your spotless flat and looked at your shorts with creases in them and your ironed T-shirt and your neat hair and, knowing your background, I thought, ha, she's rebelling against the hippie lifestyle of her youth, and is now conventional, practical, sensible, probably driven by ambition and a need to be in control of her life— was that fair?'

Clancy waved her hand in the air as if to wipe away the picture he had painted but had to agree.

'Pretty close,' she admitted, 'but what's changed?'

'What's changed?' Mac echoed in disbelief. 'What's changed? Only that you've brought home a goat, you're talking about fixing the old stairs as if you know what you're doing, and now you're channelling Hester and bringing three children you don't know into your life.'

Clancy grinned at him.

'I don't see it as channelling Hester. And where

does offering the children a home not fit with the practical and sensible?'

This time the head shake was one of pure disbelief.

'I'll go up to the annex and talk to Helen. If she's okay with the arrangement you can meet her later. Actually, tomorrow morning would be best as she tires easily and the kids are sure to have visited today.'

Clancy slid out of the car, glad to escape the force-field of attraction that surrounded Mac like an invisible cloud of magnetic impulses, and, to be honest, to give herself a little breathing space to consider her rash invitation. What had happened to her controlled, ordered life?

Mike came rushing to greet her and she pushed him off her chest and rubbed his head.

'This is all your fault,' she told him sternly, but she did go on to reveal that some little boys might be coming to stay, and from there couldn't help thinking how exciting Hester's house would be for little boys—although she'd better check the attic rooms and the widow's walk right now.

Having one of those small boys plummet off the widow's walk would be disastrous.

But better to be thinking of this change in her life and possible disasters than considering Mac's force-field. A man trailing two marriages in his wake was a dangerous proposition for a woman who'd already had one man in her life who had gone away, and another man who'd switched his love from her to her friend only weeks before their marriage.

She didn't obsess over either of these departures—well, not much—or blame herself in any way, and she was still reasonably confident that somewhere in the world there was a man for her—a stable, steady, sensible man.

It was just a matter of meeting him.

And getting over the attraction she felt towards a man with dark, twinkling eyes.

Inside the house she climbed up to the attic rooms, discovering, between the two, another set of even narrower stairs leading up into a third attic, which, from the layer of dust over everything, hadn't been explored for a while.

'I'll just lock that door and keep the key until I have time to check it out,' she said to Mike, who was accompanying her on her explorations.

Both the attic bedrooms, though small, seemed solid enough, a state Clancy tested by jumping up and down on both floors. The beds were singles but large, and each room had a cupboard for the boys' clothes and a small desk with a chair by the window. The windows opened but as far as Clancy could tell, they were too small to climb through, and even if one of the boys wriggled out, he'd land on—oh, it had to be the widow's walk.

Opposite the stairs to the upper attic was a door, and opening this Clancy found herself on the little platform—or was it a path—that had been built around these top rooms. Delighted, yet a little uneasy, she ventured out, finding it, too, was solid, and if an adventurous child *were* to climb over the railing, the worst he could do would be to slide down the roof and drop, hopefully not head first, onto the ground.

Nevertheless she might keep the key to the widow's walk door as well, until she knew the boys better.

But as she walked around the little platform, she forgot her potential guests, looking out over the countryside, seeing fields of sunflowers in the east, their faces turned towards her as the sun was setting at her back.

To the north, there rose up a row of strange, lumpy mountains, continuous except for a dip towards one end.

A gap through which a horseman could ride?

Squinting her eyes, she knew she wouldn't pick up a horse and rider, but she'd see the dust from the horse's hooves—or maybe, somewhere on one of those strange mountains there was a bare patch where a man could light a fire, signalling he would be coming, in the darkness, bridle jingling, horse's hooves drumming...

'I haven't been up here for ages. Are you sure it's safe?'

Mac's voice made her spin around—not a bushranger, but a pirate.

'Quite sure. I jumped up and down, but I think

I'll keep the door locked until I size up the degree of mischief in the boys. You spoke to Helen? Do you think she liked the idea?'

Was he getting fanciful that he thought he heard a note of tension in Clancy's voice? Was she regretting her offer?

Bit late for that!

'She was delighted—although, of course, she wants to meet you. And Tom was there as well, and he's over the moon. If it all works out, he can phone his boss tomorrow and get Tuesday's plane. That way he can be home for Christmas with Helen and the kids.'

It wasn't until Clancy moved closer and put her hand on his arm that he realised that some of his despair over this family's situation had leaked into his words.

'You're thinking it will be their last Christmas together,' she said quietly, then she put her arms around his waist and rested her head on his chest, giving him a quick hug. 'I don't think people realise just how hard it is for people like you who are involved with terminally ill patients, especially when they're friends. You mentioned Ally-sha needing a counsellor—do you have someone to talk to?'

She had moved a little away from him so she could tilt her head and look at him when she asked the question, and as Mac looked deep into those green eyes, he knew he was drowning.

He pushed away.

'I'm fine,' he lied, just as he had when Lauren had left him, and when Kirsten had taken her own life, leaving him not only distraught but riddled with guilt.

'I'm fine,' he repeated, in case Clancy didn't get the message that he couldn't handle sympathy and never had been able to.

He turned to walk away, but she wasn't going to have that.

'I'm sure you are,' she said, 'which is why you can stand and watch the sunset with me, and talk to me a little. Tell me why two women would leave a man as kind as you. And don't try to tell me you're not kind. I may not have known you long, but the compassion you showed Greg Rogers, your concern over the Lawrence family, the love you obviously had for Hester—these things aren't put on, they're real and come from deep inside what could only be a truly understanding, empathetic man.'

Before he could answer, she took his hand and led him around to the western side of the walk, to where, in a blaze of glorious colour, too rich and varied to describe, the sun was sliding behind the hills.

'I can never decide,' the person holding his hand said, 'whether I like sunsets or sunrises best.'

And the hand holding his tightened with the sheer pleasure of the moment, and he forgot all the reasons he should steer clear of Clancy and let the beauty of the heavenly light show fill his soul with peace.

Enough peace to talk a little, to tell her more things he didn't talk about?

'Talk?'

It was a suggestion, softly spoken, and suddenly he knew he could.

'I won't even be looking at you while you're talking,' she added softly. 'Start with number one.'

So Mac did, explaining how he and Lauren had been in the same year at university, both studying law, marrying early, in second year, because they were both from fairly well-known legal families and it had seemed the right thing to do.

'Then I decided to switch to medicine,' Mac said.

It was a simple enough sentence, but something in his voice must have given Clancy a clue for she forgot about not looking at him and turned to study his face.

'Why?'

He looked at Clancy, shadowy in the fading light, but he could still make out the green-blue eyes, clear ivory skin and cap of dark hair, and beyond the looks he saw understanding and compassion and decided, yes, he did want to!

'My grandfather died—the Greek one from here. I had spent all my school holidays here in Carnock with my grandparents, swimming in the river, playing around the café and the hotel, making friends with the locals. I loved the place but most of all I loved my grandfather, who somehow knew just exactly how a growing boy would feel and what he'd want to know and do. I can't explain the bond, and it probably became stronger after my grandmother died when I was fourteen.'

He paused, trying to fit things into sequence, but knowing no way he told it would absolve the guilt he felt.

'Once I started university, there were always other things to do in the long summer holidays—work experience in law firms, skiing in Japan with friends. Towards the end of fourth year my grandfather died, and I realised, to my shame, I hadn't seen him since my wedding. But it was when I found out how and why he'd died that things changed.'

'Unnecessarily?' Clancy asked quietly, and Mac nodded.

'Appendicitis, followed by peritonitis—and by the time they got him to a surgeon in Toowoomba it was too late. I hadn't even known that Carnock no longer had a doctor—Health Department cutbacks and a lack of medical professionals willing to work in the bush.'

'So you switched to medicine. Always intending to work here in Carnock?'

Mac nodded again—it was easier than talking because remembering that traumatic time in his life always brought pain.

'Your grandfather wasn't really your responsibility,' Clancy said quietly. 'It was only because you loved him so much that you felt guilt that he had died so needlessly.'

Mac stared at her, unable to believe she'd picked up on the feelings that still, from time to time, haunted him, for all his rational self knew he couldn't have done anything to save the grandfather he'd loved.

Lauren's failure to understand his reaction had been the first crack in their marriage, although it was only in retrospect he'd realised that.

He squelched the sigh that wanted to escape—right now he had a story to finish, and this was the easy part.

'Lauren wanted a lawyer, not a doctor, for a husband, so that was that as far as marriage number one was concerned. Both our families were lawyers and she'd thought we'd both carry on the tradition and our children would follow—generations of legal eagles! At least that's what she said, although, looking back, I think maybe the idea of me having another six years of study and then internship before I started earning real money might have been factored into her decision.'

'Oh, Mac!'

The woman who'd made him talk slid her arms around his waist and held him close while the spectacular blaze of colour faded to soft pinks and purples, and the pain the memories had brought back washed from his body.

Had it helped him to talk?

Clancy had no idea as she eased away from him, but, having been through it herself, she had felt his hurt and ached for him. Although she must be mad, not only to be talking to him about stuff that mattered but giving him hugs? Holding his hand?

Feeling his pain…

Poor man! All he'd wanted to do was the best he could for his grandfather's memory!

Not that it was any of her business, and the sooner she had small boys and a teenager to worry about, the better off she'd be.

And she wouldn't be here for long—just over Christmas, although that was still a couple of weeks away.

Mind you, there was no reason she couldn't stay for the whole of the school holidays if that would be a help to Tom and Helen Lawrence. She didn't need to see all that much of Mac.

Fortunately Mac changed the subject.

'Tom said he'd be up at the annex at eight in the morning—is that too early for you? He thought he could take you from there to meet the kids.'

He had moved away from her both physically and emotionally—embarrassed by the things he'd told her, perhaps—and was leaning on the railing, his back to the last light of the day so his face was in shadow. But as far as Clancy could tell from his voice, the hug and hand-holding and talking about his first marriage hadn't affected him in the slightest and life was business as usual.

'Eight is fine with me,' she responded, just as businesslike, although standing there, with the shadowy figure of Mac, was becoming more and more unsettling. Of course there wasn't a fire out there on the lumpy mountains to the north. It was summer, fire danger high...

'Go carefully on the stairs,' Mac said as she walked away from the man and her fancies.

'I will,' she told him, thinking what she really needed to do was to go cautiously in this new life of hers and be especially careful to avoid opportunities to be with him. But there was no escape right now for he was following her down and they'd need to feed the goat and Mike and fix something for dinner. The togetherness of this arrangement was far too domestic for Clancy's peace of mind.

'I'm going out tonight,' Mac announced when

they reached the bottom of the main stairs. 'Will you be okay on your own?'

'Of course,' Clancy told him, biting her tongue so she wouldn't ask where he was going. Of course, it was none of her business and, besides, it sounded too domesticated for words!

He disappeared out the front door, and some perverse imp inside her whispered, At least he didn't shower and change his clothes.

'Listen to yourself!' Clancy spoke the words aloud, scolding herself for the way her mind was working. 'What Mac does and who he does it with is none of your business!'

Clancy fed the dog, then, realising there was still enough light in the sky, she went out to explore the back yard, searching for oddments of timber thin enough to use to stabilise the wobbly stairs.

And a hammer, she'd need a hammer. There was sure to be one in that shed that looked a little more sturdy than the others.

The goat followed in her wake, Mike joining them when he'd finished his dinner.

With a hammer and seven likely pieces of wood in her hand, Clancy returned to the kitchen, where she set them down, washed her hands, then made herself a simple meal of eggs on toast. Mike kept her company, and the goat waited at the door for any leftovers.

The goat wasn't coming in, Clancy realised. She *must* have been someone's pet to be trained not to cross the threshold.

Thinking about the goat, and Mike, and fixing the steps before the children arrived kept Clancy's mind occupied for all of three minutes, after which it switched back to how firm Mac's chest had felt against her cheek, and how she'd felt the thud of his heartbeat piercing her skin to join with her own too-rapid pulse.

And how warm his hand had been, big enough to close around hers, as if her hand in his had been something fragile he had to protect—

Idiot! The man had been let down by two women—well, now she knew he'd been let down by one, and she was coming to realise, as she got to know him, *he'd* have been unlikely to have let down the second. Given that record, he'd be even more reluctant than she was to get involved again.

And she *was* reluctant to get involved again. Once trust had been broken, it was hard to mend...

She washed the plate and cutlery, cleaned the pan she'd used, tidied the kitchen, realising as she did that *she* hadn't put out a placemat for herself, then she picked up her shims of wood and headed for the staircase.

Mac drove through town and out along the road towards Heathcote—in the same direction he'd taken that morning before he'd turned back, drawn by the magnetic force that was Clancy.

But he'd played it cool, he decided, when they'd worked together at the hospital and had had lunch—and even when she'd hugged him then taken his hand to lead him around to look at the sunset. He hadn't folded her in his arms and kissed the breath out of her, which was what his body had wanted to do.

Mind you, her asking about his marriage break-up had cooled the passion, and when she'd held him after his pathetic explanation, there'd been empathy and understanding in her gesture, not heat and passion.

So, one way or another, he was controlling all the lustful impulses he felt towards Hester's great-niece, and was to be congratulated.

So why, he asked the evening star he could see twinkling in the twilight, was he fleeing in this way? By the time he reached the property his manager and his wife would have finished dinner, and although Nell would offer to feed him, he'd say no, so he'd be starving by the time he got back to Hester's house. If Clancy was still up he wouldn't be able to make himself some toast, so all he was really doing was making a complete fool of himself.

As long as he cut short his visit to Heathcote, he could get a hamburger at the café when he got back to town, which would solve the hunger problem, but solving his attraction to Clancy was a whole different ball game.

Permanently avoiding her would be one answer, but that was impossible.

Unless he shifted back to the flat he kept above the pub.

That was the answer!

But it would mean leaving Clancy with three kids she barely knew—and how happy would Helen be about *that* situation?

Having the kids stay at Hester's when he was there was one thing, but without him in residence—and with Clancy being a total stranger—it was impossible.

Arguments ran riot in his head, ideas bobbing up then being swept away by reasoning, his mind in such a whirl that he'd passed the Heathcote gate and was halfway to Thornside before he realised where he was.

He turned the car around and headed back to town—he'd eat at the café and hope Clancy would be in bed by the time he got home.

Home?

There was, Clancy discovered, a light in the cupboard under the stairs. Not much of a light, just enough to see the brooms and dustpans hanging on the wall and the shelf of cleaning fluids and bag of rags.

And a torch!

She turned it on and pointed it into the dim recess where the stairs came down to meet the floor in the front hall, and groaned when she saw the boxes stacked between herself and her goal, the fourth tread from the bottom.

The other wobbly one was second from the top—if she pulled a couple of those boxes over she could stand on them to reach it. Shining her torch upwards, she could see the grooves in the stringers and knew she could hammer in her shims of wood.

She bent low so she wouldn't bump her head and pulled a box towards her. It was full of dusty books, ancient books, the musty smell rising up to meet her because she'd disturbed them. Still, they'd make a solid base and if she put that next box on top...

Her makeshift ladder worked and she hammered her thin strips of wood home beneath the tread of the second top step, then she clambered out of the cupboard and went up to jump on the step to test her handiwork.

Terrific!

Back under the stairs, she knew she'd have to shift the other boxes before she could get to the fourth step. The next box was wooden—perhaps an old butter box like those she'd seen in antique shops. She dragged it across the floor then eased behind it, finding the last obstruction not a box at all but an old metal trunk.

It refused to budge, so she opened it, thinking if she could remove some of whatever was inside it she could make it lighter and easier to shift.

On top she found an old coat, dark and heavy, waterproofed, she guessed with lanolin from sheep wool. She dragged it out, pushing at the stubborn folds, wanting to get it out of the way so she could move the chest.

A packet fell from the folds, landing in front of where she knelt on the floor, and even in the dull gleam of the torchlight she could see the faded purple ribbon tied around the bundle.

'Letters!'

She barely breathed the word, picking up the bundle, feeling the fragility of the paper between her fingers, handling it carefully lest it all fall apart.

Edging over the coat and closer to the torch, she turned the parcel this way and that, picking out a word here and there, the lines uneven, wavering, but the faded writing—pencil?—was a beautiful, ornate copperplate script.

'Your darling man,' was all she could read on the bottom of one of the folded sheets, followed by a signature so scrawled it was impossible to make out.

Deliberately impossible, given how clear the other writing was?

Clancy's fingers moved to untie the ribbon, although common sense told her she should wait until she could set the bundle down and so limit any damage she might do to the letters.

Before that, she reminded herself, she had to fix the step.

So she left the ribbon tied, but eased one letter

out, holding her breath as she opened it, the blood rising in her cheeks as she read words meant for someone else.

The moon shines bright and full tonight, a good moon for work, but my promise to you holds, my darling, and tonight I lie beside a campfire, an itinerant stockman working with others, moving cattle to the deep valley for the spring grass. They move, restless, lowing quietly. Is it the moon they talk to? I talk to it, knowing it will be looking down on you, too, my dearest, watching over you for me. Is your hair undone, cascading down your back and over your shoulders in russet curls, making the skin on your pale breast shimmer white as milk? Are you looking at the moon and thinking of me? Will leave this in the usual place, my fingers trembling with the love I—

The page finished and rather than try to turn to the next, Clancy set the bundle on the box of books, *her* fingers shaking slightly, aware she'd read a letter not intended to be read by anyone other than the recipient.

Isabella?

Clancy had no idea, but in spite of feeling guilty she knew she would read the others. She dragged the trunk forward then clambered behind it with her bits of wood and hammer, counting the steps to the fourth, setting the torch on the trunk so she could see what she was doing, then hammering home the little bits of wood until she knew the step would no longer wobble.

Mac came quietly into the house, using the front door because the kitchen light was on. While he wasn't exactly avoiding Clancy, he'd decided it would be easier if he saw less of her.

This plan was thwarted when he entered the vestibule to find her jumping on the fourth tread of the stairs—the wobbly tread.

'Do you want to kill yourself?' he demanded, crossing the hall with long strides and grabbing her up in his arms.

He'd obviously startled her, but she recovered

quickly, laughing up into his face as he set her on her feet.

'It's safe, I mended it. I was just testing my handiwork.'

It was the laughter lighting up her face and gleaming in her eyes that did it—bewitched him!

So now he put his arms around her again, only this time not to save her from injury but to bring her close enough to kiss the smiling mouth and catch her laughter with his lips, to taste it with his tongue.

You cannot do this, cannot, cannot, cannot...

Useless words that thundered in his head while his mouth remained fastened on hers, feasting on her, drawing out the very essence of this woman he'd so foolishly brought into his life.

He touched his tongue to her lips, uncertain of its welcome, but the dusty lips parted willingly and the shudder that ran through her body excited his to the extent he should stop this kissing now.

Now!

She made a little whimpering sound and

pressed against him, her tongue now teasing along his lips as if exploring their shape and texture, touching his tongue, withdrawing, inviting him into the warm, moist cave of her mouth.

Bodies needed air—was that why she eased away, her hands, which he knew had been wrapped around his back, going to her hair, brushing at...

Cobwebs?

He reached out and pulled one grey thread free.

'What *have* you been doing?' he demanded, because he needed something other than the kiss to think about—to talk about.

Her answer was a cheeky smile.

'Apart from kissing you, you mean?'

He groaned.

'I don't know why I did that—it can't happen, Clancy, it's all wrong. I'm no good with women. I don't mean to, but I hurt them. I should have "Danger" tattooed in red across my forehead. And Hester's niece—you're the last person I could ever hurt. I can't let Hester down like that.'

He was muttering at her, words bumbling out but making little sense.

Focus!

Think!

Or escape…

'I need to do some work.'

She frowned at him, then shook her head.

'Go do your work,' she said, then she disappeared into the cupboard under the stairs, thus explaining the cobwebs but leaving him with the uneasy feeling that he'd hurt her in some way.

Clancy sat on the butter box under the stairs and tried to rationalise what had happened.

No point in trying to work out why Mac had kissed her, but surely she could figure out the reason she'd kissed him back—she who treated all relationships with ultra caution.

The letter?

Yes, it had affected her, but not to the extent that she had happily fallen into Mac's arms and responded far too enthusiastically to his kiss.

Okay, so the attraction was there—she'd felt it since their first meeting—but she'd known him for less than forty-eight hours. He could be a serial killer for all she knew.

Probably not, but definitely a serial husband—he'd admitted that—and even if the marriage break-ups were explainable, did that make it better?

And surely he'd still look back on those lost loves with regret. Possibly he still loved one or both of the women he'd been married to. Not that *his* past mattered, it was her own experience that should be holding her back and her own behaviour she had to consider.

The memory of the kiss, of his lips claiming hers, his tongue invading with such—

Enough!

She stood up and banged her head on the stairs. Smothering the yelp of pain that tried to escape, she rubbed at her head, couldn't feel blood, so retrieved the letters and crept out of her hidey-hole.

With any luck the children would be here tomorrow, and Mac's presence—when he wasn't at work or 'out'—would be diluted by their presence. There'd be no more impulse kissing going on in this house…

CHAPTER SEVEN

INTENDING to read the letters in the privacy of her bedroom, Clancy carried them upstairs, but once there, an overwhelming tiredness crept over her so it was all she could do to have a shower, wash the dust and cobwebs out of her hair and clamber into bed.

Not surprising, given the excitement of the day, she told herself, but she knew it was emotional exhaustion, too, brought on by the heightened physical awareness of being around Mac.

Tomorrow he would go back to work and she'd barely see him, she reminded herself, but as she drifted off to sleep the kiss replayed in her head and her body warmed as it had warmed when he'd held her in his arms.

Pathetic! That was her last thought, and the first word on her lips the following morning when she awoke to find the sun shining through her window, and her mind aggrieved that she hadn't dreamt again.

Seven o'clock.

She washed and dressed, realising she'd need to explore the laundry and check out the washing machine before the day was out. Her one small bag of clothes wouldn't go far. But Helen first, Helen and Tom.

The thought of someone so young trapped in a dying body was physically hurtful to Clancy as she walked down the stairs. Motor neurones were the nerves controlling voluntary movement of the trunk, limbs, speech, swallowing and breathing, and their deterioration usually started in the hands and feet. Trying to remember as much as she could about the disease certainly diverted her thoughts from Mac.

There was a drug—she had no idea of the name—that could provide a slight extension of life expectancy, she seemed to remember, but once the disease took hold of a person, their eventual death was inevitable.

The emotional toll on the family must be terrible, but how much more terrible for Helen...

'Helen can communicate with her eyes.'

The house had been so still and silent as Clancy came down the stairs, she had assumed Mac was either sleeping late or had departed, but this information, greeting her as she walked into the kitchen, told her just how wrong she was.

'And good morning to you, too,' she replied, although she knew he was telling her something she needed to know. It had been her body's reaction to seeing him there, to hearing his voice, that had made her cranky.

'I've got to get up to the hospital, I do an outpatient clinic first thing,' he explained, standing up to take his plate and mug to the sink and rinse them both. 'I'll meet you there at eight,' he added, throwing the words over his shoulder. 'It's very basic communication but she looks left for yes and right for no. She and Tom have a more complex vocabulary so he's likely to ask questions she's suggested he ask.'

He turned around, presumably in case she had

any questions, and seeing him there, outlined against the window, sent tremors of desire riffling through her body.

Control!

'It must be so hard for him,' she murmured, leaving the shelter of the kitchen doorjamb and entering the room, heading for the pantry so she didn't have to brush against that tempting body as he left the room. Breakfast cereal lived in the cupboard so it was a legitimate move.

'For all of them,' Mac replied, and the sincerity in his voice, the depth of emotion in his words sent a flush of embarrassment—shame?—to her cheeks. His mind had been totally on the family in pain, while hers had been on him.

'You're a good man, McAlister Warren,' she muttered as she picked up the cereal she'd bought the previous day, still muttering under her breath, but mainly admonishments to herself about the stupidity of attraction.

Emerging from the pantry, she was glad she hadn't chastised herself very loudly, as the man in question hadn't left the kitchen but was standing by the door, as if waiting to make sure she didn't disappear down some rabbit hole in the corner of the pantry.

'The steps are great,' he said, and *then* he departed.

'The steps are great!' Mac muttered the words over and over under his breath as he had a quick wash then headed for his car.

What he'd wanted to do—why he'd lingered—had been to apologise for the kiss, but he had an uneasy feeling that apologising for kissing someone might be the wrong thing to do—insulting to the kissee in some way.

So he'd stood there like a big galoot and said 'The steps are great'!

He'd also wanted to reiterate that the kiss wouldn't be repeated, couldn't be repeated, but those words hadn't come out either.

Because the kiss was so much in the forefront of his mind that the thought of *not* repeating it was torture?

She'd felt so right in his arms, her body soft where his was hard—very hard in places...

Blithering idiot! *All* women's bodies were soft where men's were hard. They were made that way to match each other.

As well as his and Clancy's had?

Had his wives' bodies fitted like that?

He groaned so loudly, Mike, who'd been sitting by the car, waiting to see if he was invited to accompany Mac wherever he was going, gave a little bark of sympathy. Mac reached through the open car door and rubbed Mike's head.

'I'm okay, fella,' he said. 'Just a touch of temporary insanity!'

He closed the door, started the car and drove to the hospital, hoping there'd be so many patients waiting to see him he'd have no time to think.

'Now I'm wishing people to be ill or injured—great doctor I am!'

Clancy had listened for the car to leave but heard nothing, although when Mike joined her in the kitchen she assumed Mac had departed.

She checked Mike had water, wrote a mental note to ask Mac if the dog should be fed in the morning, went to check on Dolly, who was cleaning up the thistles growing around the rubbish in the back yard, then finally sat down to eat a bowl of cereal, wondering at the same time if having three children in the house would be enough to dilute Mac's presence, considering how badly just seeing him this morning had affected her body.

If she kept busy—and two small boys would keep anyone busy—there'd be no time to think about him, or even to take note of her reactions to him. Plus there was the girl, Allysha, a teenager about to lose her mother at a time when mothers were essential in a girl's life. She would need some special care—not intrusion into her life, but somehow Clancy knew she'd have to let Allysha know she'd be there for her at any time.

Not that she could be a replacement mother. Thinking of mothers, Clancy switched to wondering when the letter she'd posted the previous day would reach her mother—and what her reaction would be.

She tidied the kitchen, and checked out the laundry. A large cane box marked 'Laundry' was sitting on the floor, filled almost to the brim with dirty clothes.

When she came back downstairs with her own small bundle of laundry she looked again at the laundry bin. Really, she had too little to use the washing machine, so she had the choice of hand washing or tipping Mac's clothes into the machine as well.

Would he be a fussy washer? Separating out coloureds and whites? From what she could see without poking through the clothes, they were mainly jeans, shorts and T-shirts, all well worn.

Underwear, of course, but the less she thought about Mac's underwear the better, until she realised he must be a boxer-shorts underwear man.

Something else for her list?

There really wasn't a list.

Disturbed by the track her mind had taken, she upended the laundry box into the machine, added her small collection, worked out the programme and the place to put the soap, and set the machine going.

Her underwear and Mac's sloshing around together!

It could hardly be *less* sexy, so why was she feeling hot?

Hospital Annex—Helen—get your mind into gear!

She'd meant to read up on MND last night but had been too whacked by all the emotion of the day. At least this morning was nothing more than a chance for Helen to look her over—Helen *and* Tom. Presumably, she would then meet the children and if they approved of her—or of the house, more likely—it could all be sorted.

Memories of her mother taking in children from time to time floated through her mind.

'You are *not* becoming your mother!' she told herself as she took the stairs two at a time to have a quick wash before heading to the hospital.

'Would that be a terrible thing?' a too-familiar voice asked, and she turned to see Mac standing in the hall.

'I thought you had outpatients,' she grouched at him from halfway up the stairs.

'Finished early and came home to see if you wanted a lift up the hill or if that would be too much for your carbon-footprint conscience to accept?'

She scowled at him then decided a lift up the hill would be good, as it had already been very hot in the back yard when she'd gone to see to Dolly.

'Two minutes!' she told the aggravating male— still unshaven—or perhaps that was the best he could do in the way of a beard...

She hurried to the bathroom, returning to find Mac jumping on the lower of her mended steps.

'You did a good job,' he told her. 'Handyman, are you?'

She smiled, because she really couldn't help smiling at the man.

'If you'd lived in as many rundown farmhouses as I have, with a group of people who had their minds on higher planes rather than planks missing in the floor and wobbly steps, you'd have learned a thing or two.'

He looked slightly shocked, but she was used to so-called normal people having absolutely no concept of alternative lifestyles so it didn't bother her.

Until he said, 'I don't suppose you can fix tiles?'

They'd reached the car and he held the door open for her.

'Bathroom or roof?' she asked, pleased to keep this practical conversation going so she didn't have to think about the flutters.

'Well, probably both but the roof is the most important. In fact, they are slate, not concrete, tiles, and Hester has a heap of them in the back yard that she's collected over the years, but there's a leak in the roof above her bedroom. I do keep a bucket in there to catch the water when it rains, but the room starts to smell mouldy in wet weather so there could be water collecting in the ceiling.'

Clancy considered the information, knowing

full well the house had welcomed her in some way and made her feel at home, and that being the case, she could hardly let it rot.

'I probably can't be fixing the roof when the boys are there, because they'd want to join me for sure, and it would be terrible if one of them plummeted to his death on his first day in my charge. But I'll have a look when I get back from the hospital. There might be a few cracked slates up there, and we don't want the ceiling coming crashing down on one of the children.'

They'd reached the hospital, but Mac showed no sign of getting out of the car, simply sitting there, frowning at her, and a very strange frown it was too. Almost bewildered…

'Well, are you coming in?' Clancy demanded, as the continued silence and the frown were making her uneasy.

'Of course,' he said in a faint voice. 'Of course I am.'

It wasn't that his first impression of Clancy had been all wrong—being able to mend steps and fix slate tiles on a roof didn't *not* fit with her being orderly, composed and in total control of her life. Perhaps it was the fire he'd felt in her response to his kiss that made him surprised she'd be able to mend a roof.

With Clancy waiting for him at the door, Mac knew he couldn't slap himself on the head, for all that's what he felt like doing. He'd be surprised by any woman calmly discussing mending tiles on a roof, wouldn't he?

Clancy on a roof?

An old, possibly rotten roof?

'Don't you dare get out on the roof without me being there,' he declared, and belatedly climbed out of the vehicle, slamming the door, something he never did.

'This way!'

The path wound around the main hospital building, through shrubs and small trees that attracted a variety of birdlife.

'You can reach the annex through the hospital but I like to come this way because it feels like a social call rather than a medical one.'

'You're a nice man,' his companion said quietly. 'People underrate nice, but it's a very good trait to have, especially for a doctor. I used to think they took it out of all the students in medical school. Year two, semester three, additional lectures in getting rid of nice.'

It was such a startling statement that in spite of already being a little late he had to stop and stare at her.

'Did you have some really bad experiences with doctors in your nursing career? Is that why you went into teaching?'

She looked surprised, then grinned at him.

'I was a theatre nurse, remember, working with surgeons, the prima donnas of the medical world. But, no, I didn't, and I'm not saying doctors are nasty. Most are polite and caring and really doing their best for all their patients, but there's often a wall—a wall they have to build for self-protection, I imagine—and I sometimes think the ordinary things like niceness can get stuck behind it.'

Mac shook his head.

'Let's have this conversation some other time,' he said, and continued on his way. But Clancy's words were niggling at him, and without even thinking about it, he could reel off the names of a dozen of his med-school mates who were good doctors but not particularly nice. Funny, yes, sarcastic, often, clever with words, most of them, and brilliant, some of them—but nice?

No, she was wrong.

'They're all empathetic, isn't that nice?'

Clancy's chuckle told him he'd spoken this last thought aloud.

'We'll talk about it later,' she reminded him, and because a smile had lingered on her lips, left over from the laughter, his mind deserted him completely...

How had she got involved in that stupid conversation? Clancy wondered as she followed Mac up a gently sloping ramp onto a wide veranda. In a shady corner, by a bank of pots with vivid sprays of orchids flowering in them, sat a woman in a wheelchair, a strong, darkly tanned man sitting in a chair beside her.

The woman was thin to the point of emaciation,

and her body twisted, but she was still beautiful, with huge brown eyes and golden-blonde hair.

'I'm Tom Lawrence.'

The man came forward, offering his hand to Clancy.

'I'm Clancy,' she responded, shaking the big, work-roughened palm and fingers.

'And this is Helen, my wife,' Tom added, taking Clancy's elbow to lead her forward.

Clancy stopped in front of Helen and reached for her hand, shaking it gently.

Mac had pulled a chair around so Clancy could sit where both Helen and Tom could see her. She sank down into it, and said, 'I know you'll want to ask me a lot of questions, but to give you a quick rundown, I'm Hester Clancy's great-niece, although I didn't know she existed until Mac came and found me. I studied to be a nurse, specialised in theatre nursing for seven years, but I was studying at the same time and became a nurse educator and now I lecture at a university in Brisbane.

'I was telling Mac I do have some experience

with children as I did babysitting jobs all through high school and paid my way through university by nannying. Back in Brisbane I actually have a pile of references, but if you want the names and contact numbers of some of the people I worked for, I'm happy to give them to you.'

Too much information, but, watching Helen's eyes, she knew it was the kind of thing Helen needed to hear. No matter how ill this woman was, she wasn't going to let her children stay with just anyone.

Clancy smiled at her.

'I think the kids, the boys anyway, would love to live in Hester's house for a little while. There are two attic bedrooms right at the top and I've checked they won't be able to get through the windows, but I think the boys would find the little attic rooms exciting. And the yard is full of junk for cubby and go-kart building, and there's Dolly the goat and Mike the dog.'

Behind her she heard Mac mutter a faint, enquiring 'Dolly?' but all her attention was on Helen, who had turned to Tom.

'Helen wants to know why you'd do this,' he asked. 'I mean, taking on three kids you don't know, it's not something most people would do.'

'She's nice,' Mac said, putting just enough emphasis on the second word to make it sound like a disease.

'I like kids,' Clancy said, 'and on top of that, not having known Hester, or even my father for that matter, I thought I should stay in Carnock for a while to find out what I can about both of them. That's hardly a full-time job, and having the kids around would be company. We can explore the house together, and Allysha might be interested in looking at old photographs with me, and checking out the stuff stored under the stairs and up in the very top attic—the one I've locked so the boys won't get into it until I've made sure it's safe.'

'It's like she's Hester reincarnated,' Mac said, and although he was perched on a chair a little behind her, she knew from his voice he'd be shaking his head. Something he did a lot, she'd noticed.

Ignoring the other things she'd noticed about Mac that had sprung into her mind, she looked at Helen, trying to judge what the woman thought.

'We couldn't pay you much,' Tom said.

'Oh, heavens! I don't want money. I'm doing this for me as well as for you. It will be fun to have some life in the old house. The house deserves it.'

Better not to mention her hope that having the children would dilute Mac's presence. She concentrated on Helen, who still looked concerned.

'What is it?' she asked. 'Something's bothering you, Helen. Do you want to think about it some more?'

Helen's eyes slid right—a no.

'Do you think the children will be uncomfortable with me?'

Another no.

'Are you concerned about one of them?'

Helen's eyes filled with tears.

'Allysha?' Clancy asked gently.

A yes signalled by those lovely brown eyes.

'Boyfriend?'

No.

'Depression?'

This time Helen's eyes wavered, left then right then a look of such clear despair Clancy reached out and took her hand.

'I will watch over her, believe me. I won't push myself on her, but I'll make sure she knows if ever she needs to talk I'll be there for her. It's only natural she's sad and frightened about what lies ahead, but I promise you, Helen, I will be there for her and help and comfort her in any way I can, and do whatever she'll let me do for her.'

She squeezed Helen's fingers, although she was relatively sure Helen wouldn't feel that physical reassurance. What she most wanted to do was cry—for this woman, for her family...

'You'll need to meet the kids,' Tom said.

'I'm going back to Hester's house now, so maybe you could bring them there. That way they can see the place, and I'm sure the boys at least will decide it will be a fun place for a holiday. There's plenty to do and with Christmas coming we'll have to put up decorations and a tree, and maybe make some gingerbread—'

'I think you've sold the idea,' Mac said, reaching out to touch Clancy on the shoulder. 'Maybe we should leave Tom and Helen to discuss it now. I've got to get back to work, but you can take the car if you like.'

The skin beneath where his hand had rested so lightly was skittering with excitement and now he was suggesting she drive his car—

'I'll enjoy the walk,' she said, and she bent to kiss Helen lightly on the cheek, but as she drew away she saw another question in Helen's eyes— movement right and left.

Indecision?

'What is it?' she asked gently, stepping back so she could watch Helen's face—watch her eyes moving from Mac to herself, Clancy, then back to Mac.

She smiled.

'There is absolutely nothing happening between Mac and me so you needn't worry the children will be witnessing any carrying on,' she assured

Helen. 'I only met the man on Saturday, and since my father walked out on my mother when I was three, then my fiancé left me less than a month before my wedding, I'm hardly likely to be interested in a man who's already discarded two wives.'

Oops! Perhaps Mac's marital history wasn't common knowledge.

Too bad. Helen had needed reassurance, and if her heart had gone into a syncopated frenzy as she'd told the lie, that, too, was too bad.

'She's right,' Mac said from just behind her. 'You knew Hester well enough to know she'd come back to haunt me if I messed around with her niece.'

Clancy knew she'd guessed correctly, for Tom had taken Helen's hand and was nodding quietly, Helen's eyelids now drooping after the stress and emotion of the meeting.

'I will take good care of your children,' Clancy promised.

And Helen's answering yes signal pleased her

so much she forgot about Mac and the skittering skin.

She was right, of course, Mac told himself as he followed Clancy along the path from the annex to the front of the hospital. There *could* be no carrying on in front of three children, and there *shouldn't* be any carrying on anyway, for all the reasons stated, now, by both of them.

Her fiancé had left her?

How hurtful would that have been? Having been the one left, not the leaver, he knew damn well how hurtful it was.

He studied the back of the woman who'd come into his life so unexpectedly and knew the embargo against 'carrying on' wouldn't stop him feeling the attraction that simmered between them. In fact, he realised gloomily, it would undoubtedly make it worse.

'Do you want the keys?'

She spun towards him, eyebrows raised.

'Mac, it's a couple of hundred yards back to the house—I'm sure I can stagger that far.'

A smile softened the words *and* pierced his

skin, arrowing into his lungs, reminding him of the idiocy of the situation in which they now found themselves. Not seeing her at all was the only answer to the attraction but she'd need help with the children so he had to be around more, not less.

'You're worried about this? About having the children?' she asked, and he read the anxiety in her drown-in eyes.

'Not at all,' he assured her, but it wasn't enough.

'Then why are you scowling?' she demanded.

'You don't know? You really don't know?'

Clancy shook her head. Back when she'd first suggested they take the children, Mac had seemed happy about it—relieved he could help Helen and Tom in some practical way.

But now?

He opened his mouth as if to explain, then shut it again, shook his head and turned to go back the way they'd come.

'You're not going back to tell the Lawrences we *won't* have the children, are you?'

'Of course not,' he muttered at her. 'The

groundsman has a bathroom in his shed out the back—I'm going there to take a very cold shower, which I suspect might be the first of many in the coming days and weeks.'

Clancy watched him march away, not really believing he was about to take a cold shower but picking up on the implications of it *and* wondering just how well *she'd* handle the togetherness that lay ahead, given the way Mac affected her every time she saw him, or heard his voice, or even, heaven forbid, thought about him.

What had they done? She done?

No, it was for the best. He didn't want to get involved with her, and she certainly didn't need another unreliable man in her life. Having the children around would stop anything from happening, the attraction would die a natural death, and she'd return to Brisbane some time in January and resume her life.

Her safe life!

Her boring life...

CHAPTER EIGHT

S<small>HE</small> strode down the hill towards Hester's house, turning her mind resolutely to the slate roof, wondering if the shed would produce a ladder.

It did, but further investigation of the roof above Hester's bedroom revealed that the easiest way to get onto it was from the widow's walk. Unfortunately, she was perched up there, pulling out pieces of cracked slate, when Tom Lawrence pulled up outside, two young boys tumbling out of the car and calling up to her, 'Can we come up there?'

'No way,' she told them, 'but later on, if you decide to stay, I'll let you pass the tiles from up on that little walkway, okay?'

Tom looked a little concerned, but the two boys were so obviously delighted he said nothing, instead holding the front passenger door while his daughter emerged from the car.

'I'm coming down,' she called to Tom, but not before she'd taken in the fact that Allysha Lawrence was going to be a beauty, and that right now she was *not* happy.

Hurrying downstairs, she met the group at the front door.

'Do you want to see the house first, boys, or would you like to go straight through to the back yard and meet Mike the dog, and my goat?'

My goat?

'We know Mike but we didn't know you had a goat. Dad said we could sleep right up in the top of the house—can we go there first?'

The boys seemed to share a sentence, one starting it and the other finishing. Tom introduced them, Damian and Daniel, seven and eight. He then introduced Allysha, explaining she was used to looking after the boys.

Clancy shook all the hands, giving Allysha's an extra squeeze.

'I'm hoping you'll let me look after the boys for

you,' she said to the teenager, 'so you get a bit of a break to enjoy the holidays with your friends.'

Wary brown eyes—her mother's eyes—studied Clancy for a moment, but Clancy recognised a faint spark of hope in them as well, although the girl shrugged her shoulders and said, 'I don't mind.'

Accepting that any trust she received from the girl would have to be won, Clancy led the way upstairs, stopping on the first floor.

'Do you want to see the boys' rooms in the attic, Allysha, or would you prefer to have a look into the rooms on this floor and decide which one you'd like? The one on this side at the front was Hester's, and Mac tells me the roof leaks there. His is opposite, then the bathroom and I'm beside the bathroom. But as you can see, there are another two, so you can take whichever one you want.'

'I'll see the boys' rooms first,' Allysha told her, and they all squeezed up the next, narrower, stairway, the boys immediately discovering the widow's walk, which Clancy hadn't locked in her hurry to greet her visitors.

'We can see all over town!' Damian yelled, while Daniel, who might prove to be quieter, raced right around the little path.

'Okay, boys, we'll go out there later when you help me fix the roof, but right now check out the bedrooms.'

To Clancy's surprise, both boys returned immediately and Clancy smiled at Tom.

'Well-behaved kids,' she said, and Tom nodded, although his face when he said, 'Helen has always insisted on good manners,' nearly broke Clancy's heart.

The boys were delighted with their rooms, and with the door to the widow's walk now locked, the key in Clancy's pocket, they left the boys checking out their rooms and went down to the floor below, where Allysha settled on a room decorated in autumn colours, the faded quilt a complicated pattern of browns, orange and gold.

'I've never slept in a four-poster bed,' Allysha confided to Clancy.

Clancy smiled at her.

'Nor me until I came here,' she said. 'I hadn't ever seen old quilts like this either. I think they've been in the family for a long time and could probably tell us a lot of stories about what's happened in this house.'

The girl's face lit up.

'I love stories of long ago,' she said. 'I'd loved to have lived when you rode horses or got about in horse-drawn carriages.'

'Or walked everywhere because you were too poor to have a horse,' her father reminded her, but Clancy was delighted with Allysha's interest.

'Once you've settled in,' she said, 'that's if you decide to come, I'll show you some old letters that I've found, and there's heaps of stuff in the attic we can go through. Who knows what old treasures we might find?'

Allysha smiled, a proper smile, so her face lit up with pleasure, the beauty that lay ahead of her very obvious.

'I think we'll come,' she said, and to Clancy's

surprise the girl gave her a quick hug. 'Won't we, Dad?' she added.

Tom nodded, and although Clancy knew he was relieved to have found a temporary haven for his children, the glassiness in his eyes told Clancy how hard this was for him.

Tom rounded up the boys and the family departed to pack their things and return in time for lunch.

'But we haven't seen the goat or the back yard! And where's Mike?' the boys protested as their father herded them to the car.

Where *was* Mike?

Clancy waved goodbye before going in search of the errant dog. Having made sure he wasn't shut in one of the yards or sheds, Clancy decided he was a dog who could take care of himself, and investigated the slates Hester had collected for her renovation project.

Selecting four of the best, Clancy set them aside, remembering her promise to the boys that they could help. They could carry two each up to the widow's walk and pass them, one at a time, to her so she could slide them into place. But while the boys weren't here, she'd have another look in the hole she'd made to see if she could find where water might have been pooling in the ceiling.

She was kneeling on the edge of the hole, her head down in the space beneath the roof, when an excited barking told her Mike had returned.

'Are you mad, going out on a roof with no one in the house to call an ambulance when you fall?'

'Where's he been?' she demanded of Mac, who was scowling at her from the widow's walk.

'At the hospital. He shares the groundsman's morning tea. But don't try diverting me, Willow Cloud Clancy. Have you no sense at all, getting out there when you're on your own?'

He looked as if he was about to climb out and join her, or at least haul her back to safety, so she put up a hand to stop him.

'I'm not an idiot, Mac. It's perfectly safe and the slope is gentle so if a tile did come loose and I slipped, I wouldn't slide far. I can't see any water pooling in the ceiling, but I noticed there's an access in the ceiling in my room, so I can get into the cavity and have a crawl around some time and check out all the ceilings.'

Mac opened his mouth then found he hadn't a clue what to say. He'd come up here, Mike leading the way, to see Clancy almost disappearing into a hole in the roof, and his heart had stopped.

'This is ridiculous,' he finally muttered at her. 'I must have been mad to go looking for you in Brisbane when a letter and the assurance that I'd look after Mike would have covered the situation for a while at least. Now I'm stuck in a house with a woman who's seducing my body just by being around, with a horde of kids to ensure nothing can happen, and it's no good trying to avoid her, because when I'm not here she's likely to be dancing on a roof, or in some other bizarre way endangering her life, which means I *have* to be here to keep an eye on her!'

Clancy had the hide to laugh.

'Oh, Mac,' she said, 'it's just an inconvenient attraction. It will go away for sure. I don't want to get involved with you and you don't want to get involved with me, so if we just live with it for a while, it should disappear.'

'You think?' he demanded, not appeased at all—in fact, growing increasingly angry at the situation. 'And what about the roof stuff? You've got to stop fixing things!'

'Yes, sir,' the wretched woman said, standing up and snapping a salute at him, so his heart stopped again in case she missed her footing and went plummeting off the roof.

He threw his hands in the air.

'I give up!' he said. 'Just don't go killing yourself in front of the kids, they've got enough trauma in their lives right now!'

He had intended to turn away after delivering this warning, but she held out her hand.

'Now you're here, just give me a hand while I get back on the walk.'

He took her hand, and all the things he didn't want to feel rose up inside him, only this time it was more than physical. Somehow, the trust she'd placed in him to help her off the roof seemed to symbolise a greater trust, and while that should reaffirm his knowledge that he was not the man for her, he had a moment of certainty that if Clancy were to place her trust in him, he would never let her down.

'Mac?'

Having steadied herself with his hand while she climbed over the walk's railing, she was now standing very close, studying him intently, a confused expression on her face.

'Are you okay?' she asked, cupping her free hand to his cheek.

His arms ached to hold her, his body heated to flashpoint, his heart raced and his breathing faltered. She was so close, inches from a kiss. Already he could taste her lips, feel the sweet heat of the moisture in her mouth. The stirring in his groin had become uncomfortable, the need to press his body to hers, to hold her close, to feel her tremble in response—

Man, oh, man, could he *really* be standing out here where half the town could see him, lusting after this woman he knew he couldn't have?

Well, she was here too.

Why hadn't *she* moved?

And if she didn't take her hand from his cheek he wouldn't be responsible for his actions.

A smile trembled on her lips.

'Not going to be easy, is it?' she said softly, then she did remove her hand, and walked away from him, leaving him to berate his idiocy in getting involved with Willow Cloud Clancy in the first place.

This couldn't be happening to her, Clancy told herself as she hurried off the walk and down the stairs, finding sanctuary in her bedroom where she wrapped her arms around her shaking body and tried to understand what had just happened.

She'd put her hand to his cheek and every nerve in her body had leapt to attention. Her nipples had grown hard and scratched against her shirt while the ache between her thighs had all but overwhelmed her.

If she'd moved her hand, stopped her skin touching his, it might have broken the spell, but it had stayed there, beyond the reach of will, while his dark eyes had clouded with desire and she'd known her own would have shown her response.

Would a kiss have helped, or made the situation worse?

She had no idea, she only knew the attraction she felt towards Mac was unlike anything she'd ever experienced—her entire body from her toes to the hair on her arms responding to the man's presence like iron filings to a magnet.

It was crazy!

Stupid!

Unbelievable!

Yet as she stood and shivered in her bedroom, she knew that it was real—only too real!

Enough of the analysis. The question was, what to do about it? She forced herself to think logically but her brain resisted logic.

Ignoring it was impossible—she got that far—and doing anything about it while the children were staying here was equally off limits—she'd promised Helen.

Maybe Mac was right and a regimen of cold showers was the only answer.

Clancy sighed, then turned her mind to practical matters. Make up the children's beds, check the pantry for food, although once the family was settled in they could sit down and discuss likes and dislikes in the food department and maybe all go shopping.

She'd need a car...

Cold showers weren't going to cut it as far as the domesticity of the situation was concerned, Clancy realised. The two boys pushed a trolley through the supermarket, Allysha and Mac right behind them, and she was bringing up the rear.

A family out shopping!

What was most upsetting was the fact that for so long this had been Clancy's dream. All through her unconventional childhood and even into her teens, her dream for her future had been just this.

'You okay?'

Mac turned towards her as she reached for a large, economy bottle of tomato sauce.

'As a child who lived on whatever happened to

be growing in the garden at the time, this was always my dream—a grown-up me shopping with my family in a supermarket, buying things to stock the cupboards in my own, real, home—sliced bread in plastic wrapping and peanut butter in a jar.'

His eyebrows rose.

'Yes, I know it's not my family and, yes, I know dreams don't come true, and, in fact, it's a good way of killing that particular fantasy, especially right now when Daniel is about to crash the trolley into that woman in red. You're supposed to be in charge of the boys!'

He smiled at her, this time without the heat she'd seen in his eyes earlier, but with so much kindness and understanding she wanted to sit down, right there in the middle of the supermarket, and cry.

'Come on,' she said to Allysha instead, 'let's go down the soap and toothpaste aisle and you can get whatever shampoo and conditioner you need and tell me what toothpaste the boys are used to.'

Allysha fell in beside her and they sauntered

off—well, Clancy hoped she looked as if she was sauntering because inside she was running for her life!

Those twinkling dark eyes of one McAlister Warren saw too much, far too much!

To Clancy's relief, Mac had to return to the hospital after lunch, so she and the boys cleaned up the kitchen, while Allysha was excused as she'd help make the sandwiches.

'Can we fix the roof now?' Daniel asked, but as soon as Clancy took them into the back yard to get the slates, the boys were so entranced she left them exploring and went up to do the roof herself.

'Are you okay?' she asked Allysha as she passed her open door.

The girl looked up from where she was lying on her stomach on the bed, a book between her elbows.

'I'm fine,' Allysha responded. 'I looked in the library and there are just heaps of fab old books. It's okay if I bring them up here to read?'

'Of course,' Clancy assured her. 'The boys are

in the back yard and I'm just going to slide these slates into place on the roof, so yell if you want anything.'

But Allysha had already turned back to her book and, being a reader herself, Clancy understood.

By the time Clancy had replaced the cracked slates and checked around the part of the roof she could see for any further damage, the boys had built a sizeable cubby house in the back yard. They'd even managed to incorporate the old door into the design.

'I'd better have a look at your efforts,' Clancy told them. 'I don't want the roof or walls falling in on you.'

The boys were pulling long grass from over the fence to feed to Dolly so Clancy bent to enter their building, stopping short inside the door when she realised Mac was already inside.

'We've got to stop meeting like this,' he muttered at her, before turning back to where he was hammering some solid-looking timber into place.

'I had no idea you were here,' Clancy retorted. 'I just came to check it was safe.'

'Did you think I wouldn't?'

He punctuated his words with blows of the hammer onto the nail head.

'I thought you were at the hospital,' she snapped, 'but as you've obviously got the job under control, I can leave you to it.'

She was about to grump her way out of the little building when he said her name.

Just a soft, barely there, 'Clancy...'

The desire she didn't want to feel trickled down her spine and although she knew she should keep walking—should get out of the enclosed space that held the man she needed to avoid—she turned back to face him.

This time *he* reached out and put *his* hand on *her* cheek.

'We mustn't let it make us bad friends,' he said. 'The kids need security. They don't need to hear us sniping at each other.'

Clancy reached up and took his hand, intending to remove it from her cheek, but somehow keeping hold of it as she lowered it to his side.

'I'm not usually a snapper or a sniper,' she mumbled, before giving in to all the mayhem that had invaded her body and lifting his hand again, pressing a kiss to the palm before returning it to him.

She watched as he closed his fingers across her kiss, then, after nodding to her, resumed his hammering.

This, Clancy realised as she emerged into daylight, was going to be a whole lot harder than she could ever have imagined.

But then she looked across to where the two boys had harnessed the dog and the goat to a rough piece of board they obviously intended using as a sled and knew that, however hard it got, she and Mac just had to see it through—to give these kids a decent break and some security in a world that was falling apart around them.

The happy-family scenario continued until after a barbeque dinner, when the boys realised there was no television set in the house. Howls of disbelief greeted this discovery.

'But what can we do until bedtime?' Daniel demanded.

'Play games?' Mac suggested. 'Or I could set up my telescope on the widow's walk and we could look at the stars.'

This won instant approval from both boys, who went happily down to the pub with Mac while he collected his telescope from his flat, before following him upstairs so he could set it up.

Clancy was feeling a little guilty that entertaining the pair had been left to Mac, until Allysha came down from her bedroom and asked Clancy about the letters.

'Wait here,' Clancy said, settling Allysha in one of the comfortable armchairs in the sitting room. 'I'll bring them down.'

She carried the bundle downstairs and put them on a small table between the teenager and herself, carefully untying the ribbon and separating the letters, most on a single sheet of paper, written on both sides.

'No one writes letters any more,' Allysha said. 'It's all texts and emails and stuff, so when people get older they won't have anything like this to look back on and read.'

'Very true,' Clancy replied, then she repeated the story of Isabella and the bushranger that Mac had told her. 'I think these letters might be from him to her.'

'Oh, that's so romantic,' Allysha sighed.

She lifted one of the fragile letters and began to read, her lips moving just slightly as she followed the words, a frown creasing her forehead where they were hard to make out.

'He really loved her, didn't he?' she said, and Clancy nodded.

'Does Mac love you like that?'

The question, coming out of the blue, floored Clancy for a moment then she rushed into a garbled denial—they'd only just met, they didn't know each other, there was nothing between them.

Had she blushed as she stumbled through the words that Allysha smiled and said, 'Oh, no?'

'What about you?' Clancy asked. Counterattack was always good. 'Do you have a boyfriend?'

'Not really,' Allysha replied, although now *she* was blushing. 'There's this one boy at school, I think he likes me, but most of the boys, well, they don't want their mates to think they like girls so they don't do anything about it. But if I'm walking home and there are no other kids around, then he sometimes walks with me.'

'Does he live near you?'

Allysha looked startled by the question.

'Not really. He lives over this way, up near the hospital.'

Clancy smiled at her.

'Then my guess is he does really like you and in time he'll get around to telling you.'

'But he probably wouldn't write me a letter like this,' Allysha said wistfully.

'Most teenagers wouldn't,' Clancy assured her, 'but when he's older, you never know!'

Allysha put the letter she'd read back into the

pile, and, realising that topic of conversation was finished, Clancy started another one.

'What do the kids in town do during the holidays? Are there things you all like to do?'

Allysha sighed.

'Most of the kids go to the beach with their families, like we used to do, but if we're in town then we swim in the river, or have picnics in the bush. Dan and Damian just muck around at home most of the time, or ride their bikes to friends' places. I like to read best of all, but since I've had to watch the boys I don't have as much time for that.'

'Well, you have to fit in some fresh air and exercise some time but now I'm here to watch the boys you can do all the reading you want. Can we get to the river on bikes from here?'

'Oh, it's easy,' Allysha told her. 'Just down the road. But we left our bikes at home. Have you got a bike?'

'Back in Brisbane,' Clancy told her.

'Then you can have Mum's, I know she wouldn't

mind. We can walk home in the morning when it's cool and ride the bikes back here.'

Clancy smiled at her.

'I can see why you've been such a good help to your father, looking after the boys and organising things.'

She gave Allysha a hug and was glad when the hug was returned.

'Can I read in bed?' Allysha asked.

'For as long as you like,' Clancy told her. 'It's holiday time so you don't have to be up early.'

'Except to get the bikes,' Allysha reminded her, then she said goodnight and went up to bed.

Mac appeared only minutes later to announce the boys had identified Mars and Venus in the sky and were sold on astronomy, but were tired so he'd supervised the cleaning of teeth and tucked them into bed.

Feeling she'd been neglecting her duty, Clancy hurried to her feet.

'I'll go up and say goodnight,' she said, only slightly relieved she had an excuse to escape Mac's company.

Daniel was already asleep, the day in the fresh air having tired him out, while Damian was drawing in a big sketchbook, doing a picture of the cubby they had built.

'Hey, you're good,' Clancy said, and he looked a little embarrassed as he admitted he loved to draw stuff.

'It's great you can do it,' Clancy told him. 'I'd love to be able to draw.'

'I could show you,' Damian offered, and Clancy gave him a hug.

'Thank you,' she said, then she kissed him goodnight, adding the information that they were going back to their house early in the morning to get their bikes, so not to stay up too late.

'Rad!' Damian replied, and Clancy took it as delight and left the room.

The country air must be getting to her because she felt tired enough to go to bed, until she remembered the letters she'd left downstairs. Aware they should be preserved, she decided she'd go down and slip each one into a zip-lock plastic bag, a supply of which she'd seen in the pantry.

When she went back to Brisbane she'd visit the museum or state library and find out about conserving them properly.

She wandered down the stairs, thinking that all in all it had been a satisfactory day, and, after retrieving the plastic bags, went into the living room.

To find Mac sitting where Allysha had sat, peering down at a letter he'd spread on the little table.

'You found these?'

'Under the stairs,' Clancy explained, sinking down into the other close chair.

'The bushranger?' Mac's smile told her he was as intrigued and delighted as she was.

'I think so.'

Mac's smile broadened as he carefully lifted the letter he'd been reading.

'The guy could write,' he said. 'Listen to this.

'I close my eyes and printed on my eyelids see your eyes, the sweet green-blue of the mountains back home. I hear your voice, soft and

husky, and am transported to a place where we can be alone, to a time when I can touch you with my fingertips, trailing them along your arm, reading the texture of your skin so I will know it even in my dreams. I long to press my lips to yours and know you won't resist my caresses. To feel your lips respond, telling me without words all I need to know.'

'Mac, stop!'

Clancy all but gasped out the words, her body so caught in the spell Mac's voice had cast about her, the spell of the bushranger's letter. The fires Mac had ignited earlier had sprung from doused embers to full flame and her body burned and ached and quivered with the wanting.

Mac's grin told her he knew exactly how the words had affected her but *his* protest, 'I'm not feeling all that comfortable myself,' didn't help.

'This can't go on!' Clancy told him, using her sternest 'student in trouble' voice.

'I know it can't,' Mac said, not smiling now.

'Let me read the next bit. *I am not worthy of you, my dearest, I know that only too well.*'

His voice was gruff enough to make Clancy's heart hurt.

'That's nonsense if you're putting yourself in the bushranger's place,' she said. 'Everything I've seen and learned about you tells me that you're a kind, concerned, generous and caring man. Anyway, we're not talking you and me, we've already settled that we wouldn't suit, but tell me why you've got this hang-up about not being husband material. As far as I can tell, your first marriage broke up because you both wanted to take different paths through life. That happens no matter how much people might love each other. No marriage would work in those conditions, not long term.'

Mac stared at her, unable to believe that such a simple explanation could possibly be correct and the guilt he'd felt about virtually cheating on Lauren, not with a woman but by changing his career, had been for nothing.

But apparently while scales were falling off his eyes Clancy's mind was on other things.

'Tell me about your second marriage.'

Had she really asked what he thought she'd asked? Right out like that?

'Well?' she demanded, so he had to assume she had.

Maybe if he explained...

'It can't have been that bad,' the woman whose eyes he'd compared to lucerne, not rolling green-blue hills, persisted. 'And even if it was, you should talk about it. I bet you haven't, not to many people, and you probably haven't because you're too busy blaming yourself for what happened.'

Could he talk about Kirsten?

That *had* been his failure, surely, and, probably because he didn't want Clancy thinking badly of him, he held back.

He looked at her, now busy doing something weird...

'I'm just putting the letters into plastic bags, which might not be the right thing to do but handling them isn't good either, and I do so want to read them. I'll leave the bags open so they don't sweat.'

She glanced up to slip him a smile.

'But you could talk to me while I do it,' she said softly, and for all his misgivings he knew he could.

'Kirsten was unstable. I knew that all along. The specialists had diagnosed bi-polar but I came to realise it was a more severe form of manic depression, a term used less these days, although it explains the highs and lows the sufferers endure far better. Unfortunately, like many people, brilliant people, too, who have chemical imbalances in their bodies, when she was well she couldn't believe she needed medication to balance things out, and, try as I might, I couldn't really keep check on her.'

He sighed, looking into the empty fireplace, remembering the highs and lows of life with Kirsten.

'Long story short, we'd only been married six months, living here in Carnock, in the flat above

the pub, when she suffered a really severe epi-
sode. I'd flown a cancer patient down to Brisbane
for a regular dose of chemo and returned to find
her dead of an overdose.'

He knew the words had come out rough with
pain and saw the hurt they'd carried in Clancy's
lovely eyes.

'Oh, Mac!'

She breathed his name and moved her hands
as if to reach out and take his—only in sympathy, he understood that. But she stopped herself,
no doubt aware where a simple touch could lead,
and with her promise to Helen still clear in both
their minds, it had been a good decision.

Then her chin went up and she muttered something about the children not being here right now,
and did reach out to grasp his hands.

'I cannot even imagine the pain you must have
suffered, or the torment that must have lived
within your wife, but if you think like a doctor
and not a heartbroken man, you must know it
was probably inevitable. Had she attempted sui-
cide before?'

He nodded.

'Although I didn't know that until later, when her parents came to the funeral. She'd tried not once but half a dozen times.'

'Oh, the torment she must have gone through to think death was the only answer,' Clancy whispered, and suddenly Mac realised how true that must have been, seeing the tragedy from Kirsten's side, not through the pain and guilt of his own reaction.

He squeezed the hands that held his, then stood up and walked away, needing time to think, perhaps to grieve again, for the living hell that must have been Kirsten's life...

Clancy watched him go, her arms aching to hold him, just to comfort him, because the bleakness in his voice had told her he was reliving the pain of the past.

A promise was a promise, she reminded herself. And then she, too, went to bed. Although not to sleep, thinking of the man she was beginning to know—beginning to love?

Surely not...

Especially not now she knew about Kirsten.

It was probably easy to fall out of love with a woman who had left you, but one who'd died? Wouldn't she still have a hold on Mac's heart?

CHAPTER NINE

THE days passed swiftly. Picnics by the river, visits to the hospital, extensions to the cubby in the back yard, and a real go-kart under construction with Mac's help.

Clancy sat on the widow's walk, watching the sunrise and thinking back over all that had happened in the past ten days.

It was Mac's interaction with the boys that showed him in a different light. So far Clancy had seen him as a kind and understanding doctor, going that little bit further with patients and their families. But with the boys, guiding their building projects, playing football and cricket with them, cuffing them lightly on the shoulder in reproof for a swear word, hugging them easily in delight for a good catch, she saw another

Mac, a Mac who would make a wonderful father for some lucky children.

Why had neither of his wives seen this and put their trust in the love they must have shared? Why hadn't they let his love help them through their differences and, in Kirsten's case, the bad times?

The man would make a perfect husband.

But not for her, she reminded herself.

It wasn't only the trust issue, but how could she live like this?

Okay, she'd invited the chaos of the kids into her life, but it was temporary chaos.

Or was it?

Didn't the slightly chaotic atmosphere in this house now make the life she'd thought she wanted—calm, controlled, ordered—seem dull and pathetic?

Not a life at all?

Couldn't this house, although very different from the home she'd pictured for years in her mind, become a home?

Not that staying in Carnock would mean she

and Mac would get together. He was, understandably, as wary of commitment as she was, for all the attraction between them.

If she stayed, he'd shift back to his flat at the pub. He'd already told her that he'd only stayed on in the house to have someone in it until she'd seen it and decided what she wanted to do. And right now he was staying on to help with the children.

Problem was, could she stay in Carnock *not* involved with Mac—seeing him around town, feeling the way she did about him?

Loving him?

Mike arrived, bounding up the stairs and out onto the walk, the grin on his face seeming to say he'd been looking all over for her and now he'd found her he was in seventh heaven.

He sat down beside her, panting happily, and she put an arm around him and gave him a hug, then ruffled his head, hard, the way he liked it.

'And as for you!' she told him. 'How could I let *you* go out of my life, for all you switch allegiance to the boys if they're having fun, or to Mac if he whistles you for a walk?'

She spoke sternly but she'd grown to love the dog, who was her constant companion most of the time, choosing her to loll beside if they were playing board games, sitting at her feet at the dinner table and lolloping beside her on Helen's bike when they rode to the river.

'You know we're going out with Jimmy's mum today.'

Two pyjama-clad boys erupted onto the walk.

'I do, and there are clean clothes set out for you on the desks in your rooms and Mrs Marks is collecting you in half an hour. So have a wash, get dressed and come downstairs. I'll fix your breakfasts.'

The colour of the sunrise had faded completely and the already warm sunshine was promising a hot day. Leaving Mike to hassle the boys, Clancy went down to the kitchen, setting out the place-mats, cereal bowls, cereal and milk, plugging in the toaster for the endless rounds of toast the boys consumed, putting peanut butter and jam on the table ready for the onslaught.

Mac had already breakfasted and left the house,

but, then, he usually did, starting early at the hospital so he could get his work done and be free most afternoons.

Well, Clancy assumed that was the reason, although she missed him in the mornings when sometimes they might have had some quiet time together.

'Have the boys gone?'

Allysha appeared in the kitchen as Clancy was finishing the dishes.

'Just left, they said to say goodbye, and Mrs Marks asked if you could babysit Jimmy on Saturday night. She said you'd done it before.'

Allysha's face lit up.

'Great!' she said. 'She pays me, and I need more money for Christmas presents for Mum and Dad. While I've been looking after the boys I've had to say no to babysitting jobs.'

'There are jobs around here I'd be happy to pay you for,' Clancy told her. 'Things like vacuuming the top attic, and dusting all the books in that library. Cleaning fee of twenty dollars an hour. Would that be okay?'

'Oh, Clancy,' Allysha said, and she put her arms around Clancy and gave her a hug. 'I can't take money from you when you're being so good to us all.'

Clancy returned the hug, then said sternly, 'Of course you can. If you don't do the jobs I'd have to get someone else in and I'd have to pay them. We'll start on the attic today. I know there's an extension lead in the shed. You get your breakfast while I find it, and take the vacuum cleaner up the stairs. Meet you up there.'

The happiness on Allysha's face told Clancy the girl had been worrying about presents for her parents, and her heart ached for the sadness that lay ahead of this young teenager. But as she got to know Allysha, she saw the strength and maturity in the girl that would help her through it.

'Can we open the boxes?' Allysha asked when she came into the attic.

'Once we've vacuumed, or *you've* vacuumed, I should say. Start going around them then I'll shift them so you can clean underneath. Run the head over them as well, to shift the dust off the top.'

Allysha worked willingly and efficiently, and when the job was done, practically hopping with excitement, she opened the first box, pulling out carefully folded gowns from long ago, pieces of tissue paper falling from the folds.

'Ugly, ugly, ugly,' she declared, setting the first three down on top of another box. 'Oh!'

She lifted out what must have been a ball gown, an elaborate confection of satin and lace.

'Would it have been a wedding gown?' Allysha asked, and Clancy looked at it again, realising that although it looked a pale yellow it had once been white and had yellowed with age.

'It could be, and it looks old enough to have been Isabella's,' she said.

'Can I try it on?'

Clancy looked from the dress to the dusty girl.

'When you've had a shower,' she said. 'Now leave it out and put the others back. Is there a theatre group in town?'

'The Playhouse Players, do you mean?'

'If they put on plays, yes. They might like these old clothes, or maybe they could go to a museum. Put them back and we'll work out what to do with them later.'

The next box was a treasure trove of old handbags and shoes, stiff with age, but a small carved box at the bottom revealed a collection of costume jewellery that Allysha also set aside to play with later.

The final box was the prize, Allysha opening it and carefully unwrapping the topmost item to reveal a spun-glass angel.

'Is it an ornament for a table?' she asked.

'Or for the top of a Christmas tree?' Clancy suggested.

They unwrapped another bundle and found a beautiful glass ball.

'Christmas decorations—can we use them?' Allysha asked.

'I think we can,' Clancy told her. 'We'll leave the rest in the box and I'll get Mac to help me carry it downstairs. We'll go out with him one day soon and find ourselves a good pine for a tree and decorate it with the old ornaments.'

Pleased with their finds, Allysha carried the beautiful dress and the box of jewellery down to her bedroom, while Clancy vacuumed up more dust, then pushed the box they wanted closer to the door, finally coming downstairs, lugging the vacuum cleaner and liberally covered in dust herself.

She had just stowed the vacuum and showered off the dust when Allysha called for help to do up the dress. The teenager was still young and slim enough to fit into it.

'You look beautiful in it,' Clancy told her, and meant every word.

'Can I wear it up to the annex to show Mum?' Allysha pleaded.

'Not right now when Mac's not here with his car to drive you. But I'll take some pictures on your phone and you can take it up to show them to your mother.'

Thoroughly pleased with herself, Allysha

pranced around the room then very decorously made her way down the staircase.

'There should be a crowd in the foyer watching you come down,' Clancy told her, and the girl laughed happily.

With photos done Allysha changed into her usual shorts and T-shirt and headed up the road to tell her mother about the morning and show the photos.

Clancy put on a load of washing—two boys went through a heap of clothes—then gave Hester's upstairs room and bathroom a good clean. So she was in a grubby state when she emerged and and ran into Mac.

'I think the smell—' she began, hurrying into conversation because she felt embarrassed that he'd seen her like this.

But he wasn't listening, cutting across her words with, 'I've just had a chat with Annabelle, who, it seems, feels just a tad uncomfortable about you being here.'

The anger on Mac's usually smiling face was unmistakeable.

Not to mention puzzling...

'"Uncomfortable"?'

'Wouldn't you think so, seeing she stole your fiancé a couple of weeks before the wedding? Here you are worming the stories of my marriages out of me, mentioning in passing a fiancé who left but failing to mention he left you for one of your best friends!'

'And you're angry because Annabelle's uncomfortable?'

Clancy asked the question with a sinking feeling in her heart and a fist clenching her stomach. Had she been right in her first suspicions that there was something between Mac and Annabelle?

How had she managed to forget that when she'd been falling in love with him?

Mac's voice brought her out of her misery.

'I'm not angry because Annabelle's upset! Why on earth would you think that?'

It didn't seem right to mention the obvious reason, so she muttered that he certainly seemed to be angry about something and turned away, wanting to stand under very hot water for a very long time and wash all this confusion away.

Not to mention the dirt!

'I'm angry for you! And angry at myself for putting you in the position of having to meet up with Annabelle again when seeing her must have brought back all the hurt she caused.'

His voice followed her, but now she understood and had to smile, turning back to him as she did so.

Mac looked at her smiling face and the anger he'd felt on her behalf faded slightly.

'Mac!'

No one, he was sure, said his name in quite the same way Clancy did, and when she reached out and touched him on the arm, he wanted nothing more than to take her in his arms and hold her close, to protect her from the man who'd hurt her, to help her forget the pain that rat must have caused her.

To love her for ever—that's what he wanted.

'Mac?'

She was frowning now and he wondered if his

thoughts had flashed across his face like printed news bites across a television screen.

'What happened between me and Annabelle was a long time ago and, really, there's no explanation for who falls in love with who—or even whom, if you want grammatical correctness. In fact, I knew almost immediately that it had been a good thing. James and I weren't suited to each other—not deep down in a for-ever-and-ever way, which was what I wanted.'

'Well, it's not right that I should have put you through meeting up with her,' he grouched, and turned away from her, afraid if he stayed he'd not only take her in his arms but probably tell her about the love thing as well, which, given his own failures in the relationship department, was something best kept to himself.

'Before you go, and while I'm still dirty, could you give me a hand to bring a box down from the attic?'

He turned and looked at her again.

'You *are* dirty! What have you been doing? And what's in the box in the attic?'

'Right now I've been cleaning out Hester's en suite bathroom. With no one using the shower, it had grown mould. And the box in the attic contains Christmas decorations. Come on.'

He followed her along the passage and up the narrow stairs, first to the attic rooms then on again into the space below the slates. A very hot space now, at midday, made hotter by his reaction to her pert little backside going up the stairs in front of him.

'This one,' she said, and bent to lift the box, but he brushed her hands away.

'I'll do it. We'll both fall down the stairs if we try to carry it together.'

But brushing her hand away meant contact, and they both stilled in its aftermath, looking at each other, the promise they'd made Helen like a heavy black shadow in the air between them.

'Where's Allysha?' Mac asked, his voice so hoarse the words came out as a croak.

'Up at the annex,' Clancy replied, and Mac thought her voice was froglike too.

But that was his last thought, because somehow Clancy was in his arms, dirt and all, and as he held her body close to his, the tension drained out of him, replaced by a gladness he had no idea how to explain.

So he kissed her instead of trying for the words, kissed her lips, her chin, her eyelids, showering kisses on her face, not daring to move lower because there was more heat in him than in the overly hot attic.

And Clancy was kissing him back, her lips finding bits of his skin, pressing against it, murmuring all the time, wordless sounds that were music to his ears.

His hands roamed across her back, feeling the flat planes of her shoulder blades, the fine, sharp bones of her spine, the padding on her backside that had teased him as he'd climbed the stairs.

'We promised Helen,' she finally reminded him, 'and anyway, this is daft. We barely know each other.'

He eased back so he could look into her face.

'I know you, Willow Clancy. You're as soft and sheltering as the tree whose name you bear, yet tenacious, too, your roots deep in the earth, so you stay upright while floods rage around you. It isn't time we need to know about each other, you know that as well as I do because we knew each other when we met, like fate had worked it out. Whether that's a good thing is another matter altogether. I'm not sure it is, my love. You know my reservations.'

She smiled and kissed his lips.

'That you're not good enough for me? That's nonsense, but I have reservations of my own, and with both of us hung up on the past, perhaps the promise we made to Helen is for the best.'

'Do you really believe that?' he asked, his voice coming out so husky he barely heard it.

She smiled at him.

'Believe the promise is a good thing right now?' she queried. 'Yes, I do, and you know it, too, because it gives us time. Without it we'd have been in bed within days of my arriving here, and sex changes things between two people, it blurs all the boundaries, and makes it hard to think rationally, and we both need to think rationally.'

He groaned and pulled her close.

'In my opinion it's impossible to think rationally when I'm anywhere near you—sex or no sex. But you do realise there are only five more days before Tom is back and the kids will go home, if only for a week?'

He saw the flush rise in her cheeks and excitement shot through him, gripping at his gut and stirring in his groin.

'The way I feel, I know one thing,' he said, trying hard to get the words he needed, 'and that's that I would never willingly hurt you, Clancy.'

She touched his cheek, a gesture he had grown to love.

'I doubt you would ever willingly hurt anyone, Mac, and that's enough for me.'

She gave him one final hug then suggested he move the box before they died of heatstroke in the attic.

Mac took the box, hope clamouring in his heart, telling himself to stop thinking about love and concentrate on the steps because one false move and he'd be in hospital when Tom came home. He'd reached the first floor when his mobile rang.

'Hospital! I'll leave the box here so I can have a quick wash before I go. I'll take it right down later,' he called to Clancy, who had stayed on the attic level to check the boys' bedrooms, pulling their quilts straight on their beds and putting their pyjamas under their pillows. She found more dirty clothes on Daniel's floor and although the bundle had missed that morning's wash, she carried it downstairs to put it into the laundry for the next load.

Determined to keep busy, if only to keep her mind off the conversations she'd had with Mac, Clancy found another box and by dint of shifting half the ornaments into it was able to transport all of them downstairs, where she washed them one by one in the laundry tub, setting them out to dry on a towel on the veranda.

'And don't you touch them,' she told Mike, who must have sensed her despair and was sticking by her side.

He looked up at her with so much understanding in his eyes, she knelt and hugged him.

Allysha returned as Clancy was getting the makings for the sandwiches out, so it wasn't until the meal was over and Allysha took the wet tea-towels into the laundry that she saw the ornaments and remembered about the tree.

'Oh, you've washed them! Aren't they beautiful?' she said. 'Can we go and get a tree now? Once the boys are here they'll want to help hang them and they're hopeless at it.'

'We need to wait for Mac and his car,' Clancy reminded the excited girl.

'John has a ute! He's only on his Ps but he's a good driver. Dad's let him drive me to the shops.'

'John the friend who sometimes walks you home? The one who lives close by?' Clancy said lightly, but inside her stomach was churning yet again.

What did she know about handling teenage relationships?

When were young girls allowed out with young men who had cars—even utes?

'Your father would be okay with it?' she asked, and was sure Allysha was telling the truth when she repeated that her father let John drive her to the shops.

'Okay,' she said, and smiled at the excitement that lit the girl's face. 'But phone him to ask if it's okay and suggest he collects you here.'

She touched Allysha's arm.

'I know that sounds as if I'm fussing, but your mum and dad have trusted me and I don't want to let them down.'

'I won't either,' Allysha whispered, and she gave Clancy a hug that went some way to dispelling her fears.

John proved to be a gangly young man, with incipient acne but a smile so broad Clancy fell in love with him immediately.

'Thank you for doing this for us,' she said, and he blushed to the roots of his tousled hair. 'Maybe you'd like to stay for dinner—we just have something simple, usually a barbeque at about six o'clock. The boys are starving by then.'

Now Allysha was blushing, too, but as she was

smiling at the same time Clancy decided it had been a good decision. She'd actually invited him to make sure they were home before dark, but hadn't wanted to seem to be putting a curfew on them.

Alone again, Clancy pegged washing on the line, checked on Dolly, who always liked a cuddle, and began to think about dinner. The boys would eat sausages every night, but maybe lamb chops tonight...

She was in the kitchen making salads to go with the barbequed meats when the tree-hunters returned with what, she had to admit, was a beautifully shaped tree.

John proved himself even more useful by searching the junk in the yard and finding a big drum they could fill with stones and sand to keep the tree upright.

'We can get some coloured paper to put around it, and a big bow,' Allysha said, and the girl's excited happiness made Clancy feel warm all through.

She left the two young people to do the decorating, although Allysha did come into the kitchen at one stage, to put her arms around Clancy and say, 'Are you sure you don't want to help?'

Clancy returned the hug and assured Allysha she was happy they were doing it.

The boys arrived home, delighted with the day they'd spent on Jimmy's uncle's farm, and asking if Jimmy couldn't, please, please, stay the night because they'd been telling him about all the things they'd been doing, and they wanted to show him the telescope and stars.

'He can share my bed, it's big enough, and I've got spare pyjamas he can have and clothes for tomorrow,' Damian suggested, and when Mrs Marks agreed, adding in a whisper to Clancy that it would give her time to wrap his presents, Clancy gave in.

'Hey, anyone home?'

Mac's voice had come from the direction of the laundry, which told Clancy he'd driven to the side of the house and was coming in that way.

'I'm in the kitchen,' she said, her heart thumping at the prospect of seeing him again for all it had been only hours since he'd left for the hospital.

'I've got a surprise for you,' he answered, taking a long time to get from his vehicle outside the laundry door, into the kitchen, which was the next room.

'Look who's here!'

Mac finally emerged, stepping aside as he entered the kitchen to usher in a woman in a long, purple and green skirt with a gold shirt hanging over it, and a waistcoat in vivid blue completing the ensemble. Long dark hair, streaked now with grey, framed an elfin face, while behind this woman, a tall man with long grey dreadlocks hovered, as if uncertain of his welcome.

'Mum!' Clancy cried, and it was a measure of the emotional upheaval of the last few days that she flung herself into her mother's arms and burst into tears.

'I knew you needed us,' her mother said. 'I did the cards and they told me to come at once. Aloe kept saying you were a grown woman and knew what you were doing, but this was so out of character for you, I just had to come.'

Clancy sniffed back her tears, disengaged herself from her mother's arms, wiped her face with her hands and stepped back far enough to look at the man—presumably Aloe.

'But I know you, don't I?' she said.

'He used to be Eric,' her mother explained, and remembering the kindly man who'd been around most of her life, Clancy gave him a hug as well, but a tear-free one this time.

'I met them up the road, they were looking for the house,' Mac now explained.

'I'll put them in the downstairs bedroom, they won't mind the downstairs bathroom,' she said, 'and just so you know, we've two other visitors for dinner, the boys' friend Jimmy and Allysha's friend John.'

The look on Mac's face was enough to make Clancy laugh.

'Is Allysha allowed to have a friend called John?' he demanded.

'Go and meet him and check him out for yourself. They're in the living room.'

'Better than the bedroom,' Mac muttered as he stalked away, though he did turn back at the door and smile at Clancy. 'I'm assuming the rule applies to him as well.'

She had to laugh, then she turned back to her mother, wanting to hear all the news, glad somehow that her mother was here to share Christmas with her—with them...

CHAPTER TEN

EVENTUALLY everyone was fed, the dishes were done, the boys, John included, were playing Monopoly with Eric Aloe as the banker. Clancy's mother, Ellen, was teaching Allysha to read tarot cards, and Mac had disappeared, perhaps back to the hospital, although his departing without an explanation had left a little wedge of worry in Clancy's chest.

She thought back to the strange conversation she and Mac had had in the attic, the heat up there only rivalled by the heat that had throbbed between them.

She kept thinking that it was love, but surely love happened more slowly.

And Mac?

She knew he was a good man in the truest sense of the word, but, given the way two women had hurt him in the past, wouldn't he shy off any permanent commitment?

And could she handle anything less with Mac?

Then there was Mac's commitment to Carnock.

If, and it was a huge if, they *did* become involved, was this the life she wanted?

An old house—again!—a dog, a goat, people popping in and out—where was her dream of calm and order and control?

Feeling battered by the emotional rocks on which she seemed to have thrown herself, Clancy escaped to the widow's walk, with Mike coming along for company.

'If you look at it honestly, we hardly know each other,' she told Mike, 'so surely I shouldn't be so confused.'

She rested her head on Mike's shaggy coat.

'Should I?' she asked.

'Of course you should.'

Mac sat down on the other side of her and put his arm around her, and Clancy was sufficiently confused and startled to let the arm stay right where it was.

It was a warm arm, slightly heavy, but comfortingly heavy.

'You're whipped away from your nice ordered life, the one you'd decided was just right for yourself, and landed with a dog, a house that's falling down, three kids and a boarder you've promised not to kiss, although you find yourself wanting to all the time.'

The teasing note in his voice was matched right there in his smile.

'Anyone would be confused!' he added, holding her just a little bit closer.

'It's all your fault,' she reminded him.

'No, partly yours for promising Helen,' he insisted. 'And remember you're not the only one suffering from the "no carrying on" ban. Here beside you is a man in agony.'

Even as he said it, he knew he was cheating, because he was appealing to her need to comfort and help people, a need he found mind-blowingly attractive while realising it could lead to continued disruption in his life.

She turned towards him, moving a little to escape the arm he'd had around her but touching her hand to his face.

'I'm sorry,' she whispered, and suddenly he couldn't keep up the pretence.

'Oh, Clancy,' he murmured, wrapping both arms around her this time, though it meant pushing Mike out of the way. 'You really need to harden that soft heart of yours. It's because you're so trusting and giving and generous with your affection that I worry about getting involved with you. You've already suffered enough from men who went away, so how much more would it hurt you if *I* let you down as well?'

To his surprise, the woman in his arms snuggled closer, presumably forgetting the ban on any carrying on because she kissed him and having kissed him whispered against his lips, 'You could never let me down.'

And so they sat, arms around each other, as the stars twinkled above them, and the moon rose to cast a silver light across the land, and below them, in Hester's old house, various assorted beings went about their business without a clue that their hosts were very close to breaking a promise.

Various assorted beings!

Clancy eased herself away from him.

'Mind you, there's a new test for us now, with my mother arriving,' she told Mac. 'Apparently they've come for Christmas, and if you had trouble barbequing slices of tofu for their dinner tonight, wait until you meet my mother's nut-loaf turkey.'

Mac looked at her in astonishment.

'Do you really think anything your mother is or does could put me off loving you?'

'Loving me?' Clancy repeated.

'Of course I love you. Haven't I told you that?'

Clancy cuffed him on the shoulder, the way he cuffed the boys—gently and with love.

'You know you haven't. But isn't it too soon to talk about love? Might it not just be attraction?'

He put his arms back around her. 'It isn't attraction that makes me want to hug you when I see you listening to Allysha talk about the boy she likes, listening and caring and letting her see you care. It isn't attraction that makes me want to kiss you when you hug a dirty little boy who's had a fight with his brother. And it certainly isn't attraction I feel when I see all the manifestations of the Clancy you've tried very hard to hide behind your careful Brisbane lifestyle, the Clancy whose heart goes out to everyone, even wounded goats.

'It's love, Clancy, and although you know my doubts about being good enough for you, I love you and I promise you I always will.'

Clancy let the words settle around her heart, the poor fragile heart that had taken such a battering lately. She felt their healing balm and knew she should respond, but right now she wanted nothing more than to bask in the fact that Mac loved her.

'Clancy!'

The childish voice rose clearly into the night. Mike barked in response and three small boys erupted onto the walk.

'We were looking everywhere for you,' Daniel complained. 'We told Jimmy about how you make a chocolate drink with marshmallows in it and Aloe said he doesn't know how, and Ellen said to ask you—'

'I think we'd better all go down to the kitchen,' Clancy broke in before the conversation became even more complicated. She'd dropped her arms and shifted apart from Mac when she'd heard her name, and he'd stood up and moved a little away so now she turned to him.

'You'll stay here with the boys while they show Jimmy the telescope?'

'There's absolutely nothing I'd like better,' he said, grinning at her to confirm just how big a lie that was!

Clancy hurried down to the kitchen, her body filled with a warmth she'd never felt before. Yes, there was more than a little frustration mixed in with it, but she knew, in time, all would be well.

'Oh, there you are,' her mother said as she came in. 'Allysha and I were about to make hot chocolate for the boys.'

'All the boys? Including John and me and Aloe?' Mac asked, smiling at her in such a way she thought her so recently mended heart would break again but with happiness this time.

'And when you've done that you have to come

and see the tree,' Allysha said. 'And tomorrow, if it's okay, could we get some other decorations— you know, lights and stuff for the house?'

'We could put lights around the widow's walk,' Daniel suggested, 'and maybe one of those blow-up Santa Clauses up there so people could see it from the street.'

'Normal service is resumed,' Mac said quietly, smiling at Clancy across the chaos in the kitchen. 'And leave the lights and decorations to me, boys,' he said. 'My manager down at the pub has spent a fortune on lights and decorations over the last few years. We'll go down tomorrow afternoon and liberate some of them.'

'Can I come?' Jimmy asked.

'I'd like to help, too,' John put in, and Clancy laughed as she realised she seemed to have acquired two more boarders in her house.

Her house!

Could it really become *her* house?

By Christmas Eve the house was decked with lights, a blow-up Santa clung grimly to the roof, plastic greenery ran around the veranda railings and paper bells and streamers fluttered below the ceilings. Allysha, as part of a paying job, had stood on the dining-room table and cleaned the chandelier, so it gleamed and glistened when lit, shining on the table ornaments they'd found in the box of Christmas decorations.

She'd also insisted on setting the table, the boys helping, putting out not only cutlery but bowls of fruit and nuts, Christmas crackers in every place and beautifully scented white frangipani flowers scattered all around.

'Because Mum always did that,' she explained, 'and her Mum did it before her.'

Tom came home, and although the children were happy to return to their own home with him, and to have his company for the week he was off work, Clancy invited them all for Christmas lunch, telling him Mac had already arranged to bring Helen down from the annex so the family could be together.

'So,' Mac said to her as they sat on the widow's

walk late that night. 'The children are gone—does our promise to Helen still hold?'

'Temporarily gone,' Clancy reminded him. 'And my mother's still here, remember.'

'So no carrying on?' Mac whispered as he delved his tongue tantalisingly in and out of her ear.

'Not much,' Clancy managed to say, before he took her breath completely, kissing her with so much passion she responded without hesitation, hoping to reveal all she felt for him because words could only say so much.

'We're like a couple of kids kissing in the back of a car,' she said, rather breathlessly, when they drew apart.

'We both have beds downstairs,' Mac tempted. 'Big beds!'

'I know,' Clancy breathed, snuggling close to him. 'But it wouldn't feel right.'

'I know it wouldn't, my love,' Mac told her, kissing the top of her head now. 'But when we do eventually make it into one of those big beds, don't expect to get out for, oh, at least a week.'

Clancy laughed.

'We'd starve to death,' she said, and Mac held her close.

'Oh, but what a way to die,' he whispered, his lips closing in once again on hers.

'Let's read the rest of the letters,' Clancy suggested, knowing if they kept kissing anything might happen—probably would happen…

With Mike tagging along behind her, she led the way down to the comfortable sitting room, where the tree, alive with its fragile glass ornaments, seemed to shed a blessing on the room.

Together they sorted through the pages, marvelling at the writer's ingenuity in finding paper, for some were on brown wrapping paper, some on butcher's paper, while many pages looked as if they might have been torn from the front or back of printed books.

'This is the one I want,' Mac announced, picking up a cushion off the couch and sitting on it on the floor at Clancy's feet.

'My Darling,' it begins.

'The time has come to ask the question, although I know full well it is beyond bold of me to even think of asking, but things between us, spoken and unspoken, have given me hope, and now I must find the courage that I need to ignore my misgivings and throw myself on your mercy and beg that you will be my wife.'

Mac paused, and Clancy held a hand to her fluttering heart. It was a letter from long ago, nothing more, yet Mac had paused and now was looking up at her.

'Well?' he asked, dark eyes serious, fixed on hers.

'Well what?' she whispered, her lips so shaky she barely got the words out.

'Will you take the risk, my darling? Will you be my wife?'

Emotions churned through Clancy's body, while the words, all the words, chattered in her head. Control, she reminded herself. Think!

'You *are* reading the letter?' she begged, hoping he'd say yes and she could halt all the confusion.

'What do you think?' Mac said, and now he smiled, the glint back in his eyes.

The glint only made things worse. Clancy shook her head, and finally her state of shock must have communicated itself to Mac, who took both her hands in his.

'Like him, our bushranger we assume, I know I am not good enough for you. I've made a hash of two marriages, so it's with more than just misgivings I'm asking you to marry me. But if you agree, I promise you, my darling, that I will do everything in my power to make you happy every day of your life and to ensure our life together is as blissful as I suspect the bushranger and Isabella's was. I know you have your career. I could probably get a job in Brisbane. In fact, I'm sure I could. We'd need a house with a yard for Mike, and we could rent this place—the rent would keep him in dog food for life.'

She freed one hand to rest it against his cheek.

'Oh, Mac, you talk such nonsense. Live in Brisbane? You took up medicine so you could be Carnock's doctor, so why would you move?'

A half-smile moved his lips but it was such a pathetic effort Clancy had to kiss him, so it was quite a while before they got back to the discussion.

'Anyway,' she said, 'I'm not that crazy about lecturing for ever. I can do the next semester from here, because the students pick up the lectures off the internet, and I can go down to Brisbane for a week now and then for hands-on tutorials. That gives the university time to fill my position.'

'You'd stay in Carnock?'

Mac sounded so surprised Clancy had to laugh.

'Why not?' she asked. 'I like the place and even if I didn't, the man I love is here, so where else would I be? And if you think I might get bored with it, like Kirsten did, then just consider the work that needs doing on the house, and the research I want to do on my family.

'And somehow we'll have to fit in a breeding programme so we'll have enough descendents of the Heathcotes to run the property, not to mention the kids we'll have to have to run the café and the pub and carry on the Warren tradition of being the town doctor, and town lawyer.'

Mac's response was a tight hug, and from the muffled noises he was making with his face buried in her neck, she kind of thought he might be happy about her answer.

'You'd really take the chance on me? Marry me?' he finally asked, as Mike pushed his way between them, demanding attention—or perhaps reminding them of the promise.

Clancy reached over the dog to kiss the man she loved—to answer him with a kiss.

'It's no chance at all, you stupid man,' she whispered. 'Everything I know about you tells me you're the most caring, giving, loving man I've ever met. Of course I'll marry you.'

He reached up to pull her head to his and kiss her lips.

CHAPTER ELEVEN

THE meal was over, the table cleared and dishes done when Clancy and Ellen joined the others in the living room. Helen sat by the tree, Allysha by her side, lifting the ornaments one by one to show her mother the intricacies of the beautiful pieces. The two boys sat on the floor by her wheelchair, playing quietly with twisty puzzles they'd found in their crackers, Aloe cross-legged beside them, helping without interfering.

Tom was in an armchair close by, and although Mac was talking to him, Clancy knew Tom's eyes were on his family. She went across and kissed his cheek.

'You know we'll always be here for you and the kids, whenever you need us,' she murmured, and received a quick squeeze of her hand in return, but it was Ellen who surprised everyone, pulling a chair across in front of Helen and sitting down on it.

'I think the kids have probably told you about me,' she said to Helen, 'and they've certainly told me plenty about you, and what a wonderful, caring mother you are to all three of them. I know you can't do much at the moment and that's why Aloe and I wondered how you'd feel about us shifting our campervan to your place— and camping there for as long as Tom and the kids might need us? We could help out around the house and yard so when Tom's home he can spend all his time with you and the kids. What do you think?'

Helen's eyes went to Tom immediately, and Clancy guessed, from the broad grin on his face, that Aloe and Ellen had already discussed this with him.

But it was the reaction of the two boys that appeared to seal the deal. They leapt to their feet, dragging Aloe off the floor.

'You'll come and live with us, like a grandpa? Play Monopoly with us every night and teach us how to do card tricks?' they choursed, and Helen's eyes signalled yes, a tear-bright yes, but definitely assent.

'So, that leaves just you and me,' Mac said, when the Lawrence family had left to return Helen to the annex and Ellen and Aloe had taken their van to its new home.

'Seems funny, doesn't it?' Clancy said, moving into his open arms. 'We've had so many people around, the house will seem empty now they've gone.'

'Don't feel you have to fill it up again just yet,' Mac growled, bending his head to kiss her on the lips. 'This is us time, remember. Time to test the big beds.'

Which it would have been, had not Mike come bounding in, obviously in search of company now the boys had gone...

* * * * *